SHORT STORIES FOR THE RED STATES

Dominique L.

iUniverse, Inc.
New York   Bloomington

Short Stories For The Red States

This is a work of fiction. All of the characters, names, incidents,
organizations, and dialogue in this novel are either the products
of the author's imagination or are used fictitiously.

iUniverse books may be ordered through booksellers or by contacting:

iUniverse
1663 Liberty Drive
Bloomington, IN 47403
www.iuniverse.com
1-800-Authors (1-800-288-4677)

Because of the dynamic nature of the Internet, any Web addresses or
links contained in this book may have changed since publication and
may no longer be valid. The views expressed in this work are solely
those of the author and do not necessarily reflect the views of the
publisher, and the publisher hereby disclaims any responsibility for
them.

ISBN: 978-1-4502-4911-9 (sc)
ISBN: 978-1-4502-4912-6 (ebook)

Printed in the United States of America

iUniverse rev. date: 08/20/2010

Dedicated to my parents who gave me morals and principles, my cats who give me joy and peace and especially to God Who gives me everything

THE BOYS FROM THE INTERNET

January 1, 2000 1:17 a.m.

We had just returned from an intimate but very elegant New Years Eve dinner party with a few friends. Like so many others, we chose to begin the New Millennium on a very low key note. (I know the New Millennium didn't officially start until the following year, but most Americans preferred to ignore this small detail). Sebastian, my adorable husband of 11 years who I had promised to love and cherish forever (and was actually doing an amazing job of both) had just announced that he was feeling bizarre and would sleep on the couch.

January 1, 2000 2:05 a.m.

After tossing and turning for far too many times, I decided to make myself some hot tea. It had always soothed me as a child, and it would also enable me to check on Sebastian. Hopefully he was sleeping, so I'd try to fumble through the rooms without turning any lights on. Alas, I heard voices. No…make that one voice. Sebastian was talking to? Himself?

A ghost? Oh, probably our dog, Nicodemus. It couldn't be Heroditus, our cat, because he was soundly sleeping in our bed which is what I wished I was doing. As I crept in the living room I encountered one of those "defining moments" in our lives that we would prefer not be defined. Sebastian was on the phone purring I love you to whoever was on the other end of the line. It definitely wasn't the operator nor 911.

January 1, 2000 2:30 a.m.

What happened after that was not pretty and is also somewhat of a blur, partly because I was in a rage and partly because that 6th glass of champagne at dinner probably should not have happened. Anyway as my life flashed before me, Sebastian was blabbering on and on about how sorry he was and he never meant for it to happen and I had been a wonderful wife and didn't deserve this blah blah blah and he had fallen in love with Derrick before he even realized what had happened and blah blah bl…HE HAD FALLEN IN LOVE WITH DERRICK?! I really should have stopped with the 3rd glass of champagne!

"What did you just say? You're in love with whom?" I think I was screaming but can't be 100 percent sure.

"Cynthia, lower your voice. You heard me correctly."

"No, I don't think so. I thought you said you were in love with some guy named Damon. See I had too much champagne tonight and…"

"Cynthia, you heard me correctly. I'm in love with Derrick. I'm so sorry."

"Sebastian, that sounds like a guy's name. Why do parents do that to kids? Poor Darryl (not that I had any pity at all for her) going through life with a guy's name. No wonder she ended up a slut."

"She's not a slut—I mean he's not a slut. He is a guy. Please don't make this more difficult for me than it already is."

"Oh. Sweetheart, I'm so sorry. How thoughtless of me to

make this difficult on you!" (said with as much sarcasm as I could muster in my inebriated state)

"Cynthia, I didn't realize it had happened until I was already in to it."

"You already told me that once, and stop beginning every sentence with my name. You're so freaking melodramatic! So I guess I have to ask that cliché question, did you just wake up one day and discover you're gay?"

"Of course not. It's taken me years to come to terms with this."

My semi-adorable husband had taken years to come to terms with something that I was forced to come to terms with in a matter of seconds. How unfair is that?

"Anyway", the unbearable bastard continued, "Derrick and I thought perhaps you might want to move out and let us have the house so it wouldn't be so traumatic for both of us to have to move to a new place".

"Darren and you were thinking wrong, pisshead!"

"His name is Derrick, and I know you're sublimating your hostility by calling him the wrong name."

"God, Sebastian, you just saved me $5,000 in psychiatric bills. How can I ever begin to thank you?!!"

I think with that last pathetic attempt at wounding him, I passed out. Every half hour or so I woke up to what I hoped was a nightmare. No such luck!

IN THE BEGINNING THERE WAS DIVORCE— AND IT WAS NOT GOOD!

God is a pretty amazing dude because he/she/it created the entire universe in just seven days. My divorce from Sebastian took seven days plus 12 months. Life has become way too complex. Sebastian wanted to divide everything evenly which was fine with me. The only problem was he wanted me to accept a ridiculously low price for our home because David (yes I'm still sublimating my hostility) was having an allergic reaction to the fabric in their bedroom drapes in their apartment, and Sebastian was eager to move into (I guess) a drape free home somewhere. Here was a typical conversation:

Sebastian: "Tomas (the real estate agent) just faxed me some new comps and they clearly show prices are getting soft."

Me: "How about your dick? Is that getting soft too?"

Sebastian: "You really need to see a new shrink. I cannot believe how nasty you sound all of the time."

Me: "I don't trust Tomas. I think he had a thing going with Daniel before you met him."

Sebastian: "If you don't start calling Derrick by his correct name, I'm hanging up on you."

Me: "Perhaps we should get a new realtor—one who Dennis hasn't boinked."

Click. Sebastian hung up on me. Undaunted, I dialed him back.

Me: "Hey, you didn't give me a chance to ask how Donald is."

Click. Sebastian hung up on me again. This time I didn't call him back.

In the end, I was so tired of talking to Sebastian and the attorney and Fleming (our new realtor) that I sold for less than what the house was worth, but not what Sebastian and what's his name were pressuring me into selling it for. So fast forward one year, 500 empty tissue boxes and three psychiatrists later and we are now in…

January 2001

One of the first things I did upon moving into my very tiny cottage home near downtown Huntington Beach was to buy some beautiful fabric that Window Treatments R Us had significantly discounted because they were discontinuing that color I had never actually sewn anything before, but I knew that I could do anything I put my mind to. After all, in the past year I had consumed approximately 75% of the food sold in Orange County grocery stores and had not gained one ounce (there is something to be said for stress after all—it keeps you skinny). One of the other first things that I did was to call a matchmaker that I saw in the yellow pages. We set an appointment to meet in three days, and the pressure was on to get those window treatments done before I started having men over. To make an extremely long story short, I ended up having a seamstress make my window treatments which cost me double what I would have paid if I had just bought the damn things in the first place, and the matchmaker wanted $3,300 to set me up with 7 guys. That averaged out to $471.43 per guy. Not interested! Well she could offer me a special introductory offer of $2,500 for 5 dates. Even though math has never been one of my strong subjects, that averaged out to even more money. Right before I slammed the door in her face, she gave me the business card of an associate who had not been in the business as long, but could probably match me up with some wonderful gentlemen for a more cost affordable amount. On my way home, I treated myself to a hot fudge sundae which came to $4.95 with tax. I felt happy and was starting to wonder if I should just spend my money on hot fudge sundaes instead of meeting men. By my calculations I could eat 500 sundaes and be happy for approximately the same amount of money as meeting a measly five men. After my tenth hot fudge sundae in less than two weeks, I started noticing my clothes fitting a little tighter than normal. I also started noticing that my queen size bed seemed to be shrinking into a twin bed. Was Heroditus shrinking because I obviously wasn't? Ok, I had to admit I was lonely and horny and the hot fudge sundaes weren't working for me. Time to call matchmaker lady #2. Since I had no window treatments to work on and she apparently wasn't swamped with clients, we set up an appointment for that same afternoon. When I arrived at her "office" (a 250 sq. ft. room with a folding chair and itsy bitsy desk) she greeted me with an unenthusiastic "shut the door behind you, please" and pulled out a number 2 pencil and began to write. Getting a very bad feeling already! She turned out to be quite the conversationalist, this matchmaker lady #2. Here's a sample:

Matchmaker Lady #2: "So, what brings you here today?"

What I actually said: "I was hoping you could match me with some nice men to go out with."

What I actually was thinking: This chair is so uncomfortable. Couldn't she splurge for at least a cushion for it?

Matchmaker Lady #2: "I see."

What I actually said: "Can you explain how you go about finding these matches? Can you tell me a little about your company?"

What I actually was thinking: I wonder if I'm doing damage to my butt by sitting in this God-awful chair?

Matchmaker Lady #2: "I send feelers out to my contacts."

What I actually said: "Did I catch you at a bad time because I feel like there's a communication breakdown here."

What I actually was thinking: My ass cannot handle one more minute on this chair.

Matchmaker Lady #2: "No."

What I actually said: "Look, I'm not feeling very comfortable here."

What I was actually thinking: I'm not feeling very comfortable here.

Matchmaker Lady #2: "I see."

What I actually said: "You see the thing is my ass is killing me on this chair, and you're a total bore so I think I won't take up any more of your time!"

And that was exactly what I was thinking too.

Just to prove that I was not a quitter, I called a third matchmaker lady who actually had an article written about her in the View section of the Register. Her office was a little more plush than matchmaker lady #2 (there were 2 chairs with some padding in them and her desk was slightly bigger). Personality wise—no competition! She had to be competing for Miss Bubbly 2001. Normally, I'd find that annoying, but I was in an especially good mood that day because the third time is a charm and I just bought a sexy new pair of strappy sandals so the world was my oyster (I don't actually like oysters, but you get the point). Anyway Matchmaker Lady #3 told me how great it was to meet me in person and what a lovely face and figure I had and there was a whole new world about to open up to me. She just needed to ask me a few simple questions, and I was on my way to meet the perfect man for little old me.

Matchmaker Lady #3: "Describe your dream man to me. And don't leave out the teensiest detail, okay sweetie?"

Normally I do not allow strange women to call me sweetie, but as I said I was a happy girl on this particular day.

Me: "I don't really have a good concept of him. To begin with I'd just like to meet someone that I had some chemistry with. I'd like to meet someone to have some fun with."

Matchmaker Lady #3: "Of course, sweetie, chemistry is very important initially. But what qualities would a man need to have, or should I say what physical attributes would he need for you to feel that spark?"

With the word "spark" she winked and heaved her enormous breasts up and down in the most bizarre sort of way.

Me: "I just don't know. If I see him and I click then I can tell you. I was married so long and I kind of was used to my husband so I never really thought about other men, you know?"

Matchmaker Lady #3: "That is sooo sweet. Some women

are bitter about their ex's, and I just love, love, love your honesty and innocence. Oh, sweetie, we are going to find you so many great men, you're not going to be able to choose!"

Me: "Wow, that's the best news I've heard in a long time! When do we start?"

Matchmaker Lady #3: "Well, of course, there is the matter of my fees."

Me: "Of course."

Matchmaker Lady #3: "Normally I charge $4,000 for 7 men, but this week I'm having a special introductory offer of only $1,900. Would that work for you?"

Me: "Guys are on sale this week?"

Matchmaker Lady #3: "Oh I just love your humor, sweetie. You are going to be a winner out there on the dating field."

Me: "So this is like football?"

Matchmaker Lady #3: "Well, I don't know. Can you take on an entire team at once?"

At that she winked and did the boob thing again and broke into hysterics. Anyway I decided to give it a try. It did seem like a bargain at $282 plus odd change per man, and they were all going to be fantastic! It might not make a football team, but maybe soccer? I didn't know much about professional sports so I wasn't sure. Sebastian didn't follow sports at all which should have been my first clue that something wasn't quite right with the old boy. Anyway, as I drove home I wondered how I was going to juggle seven different guys chasing after me. I had to stay home at least one night a week for laundry and grocery shopping and playing with Heroditus. (Sebastian got custody of the dog in the divorce) so some poor slob was going to have his heart broken, but it couldn't be helped. A week later Matchmaker Lady #3 called and told me she had a really exciting man who would be perfect for me. His name was Clive and he was 52. She mentioned a lot of other details, but I was still stuck on the name and the age. How could I go out with someone named Clive? Even though I was now in my early 40's, I looked and felt young and did not want some old dude who probably couldn't get it up anymore taking me out. I mentioned this to Matchmaker Lady #3 (in more polite terminology) and she assured me that he absolutely did not look his age and I would adore him. She set up the date and time for us to meet for a cocktail and asked me to give her a call and let her know how it went the very second I arrived home from the date. I was in a quandary on how to dress. Should it be simple, sexy, sporty, feminine, fun-loving, conservative? I ended up having the problem solved for me because I worked overtime and did not have time to go home and change (nor feed Heroditus) so I ended up wearing my business suit. She described Clive as 6'1", fit, brown hair and hazel eyes. She had two of the four correct. Matchmaker Lady #3 and I had different conceptions of the word "fit". Hers was 25 pounds overweight with a beer belly that would make a biker proud. Hair was also a disputed term, because he had a few strands left on top which he attempted to comb over his forehead. I stayed as long as I possibly could and made some excuse about having a long day and left Clive alone with his third Heineken. I did not wait even one second to call my matchmaker lady. Her answering machine was on, so I left her a message. "Hi, this is Cynthia Mills. And I guess the only comment I have about Clive is 'you have got to be kidding'. I realize it's my fault because I couldn't really tell you what I wanted and I guess I still can't. But I can tell you what I don't want and that would be Clive or anyone remotely like him." When I arrived home, Heroditus had decided to punish me for not feeding him at his normal time and had eaten half of my ficus tree and threw it up on my new white down comforter. Ok, I'm bummed but tomorrow is a new day and Matchmaker Lady #3 would provide me with someone really great next time. As it turned out, next time never came. I called her three times before she finally returned my call.

Matchmaker Lady #3: "Sweetie, I'm so glad to hear from

you. I'm still searching for that perfect man, and I know he's right around the corner. Just be patient."

Me: "It's been three weeks since Clive. I guess it never occurred to me to ask how often you'd be matching me up. But the thing is my biological clock has already ticked and every morning I wake up with a new wrinkle and grey hair, so I'm kind of on a deadline here."

Matchmaker Lady #3: "Sweetie, you are just hysterical. I love you to death! Give me another day and I promise, promise, promise I'll have someone perfecto Garcia for you."

I didn't know what perfecto Garcia meant, but I could wait another day. When four days went by and Mr. Perfecto didn't arrive, I called her and left the following message:

"Hi, it's Cynthia Mills. Just wanted to let you know that I've instructed my credit card company to not put the charge through for your services. Thanks for all your help (said as sarcastically as I could) and have a great matchmaker life, sweetie." (again huge emphasis on the sarcasm).

So that was it. The wrinkles and grey hairs were going to go forth and multiply but I wasn't. Talk about being bummed! I looked at my sexy strappy sandals that would never entice a man into my boudoir. Probably I should return them and spend the $150 on a hearing aid which I would undoubtedly need very soon. Or maybe I should get a rocking chair and crochet an afghan. Problem was I wasn't sure if afghans were crocheted or knitted or macramed. I wasn't much of an artsy craftsy person. Stick with the hearing aid, Cynthia. After three days of total depression, I received an email from my niece in Baltimore telling me that she read an article that the internet was the new "in" way to get dates and why didn't I give it a try? The internet!! Why not just go out to the pasture and shoot myself now! Everyone knows that the internet is for losers. Everyone knows that the internet is full of perverts and married men. Everyone knows that the internet…….let me explain why I put an ad on the internet. The day after getting the email from my niece, I was watching a PBS special on beauty and they talked about dating and how very in vogue it now was to meet dates via the internet. Well if PBS was sanctioning it, then it had to be all right. So two days later my ad was up there for the whole world to see. It took me another three weeks to get a picture that was properly formatted on the ad, so the dating was slow at first. As every savvy internet dater knows, you get eight times more hits with a photo. So my life was headed in a new direction. I was on the information highway cruising for a honey.

WHY NICE GUYS FINISH LAST

Before my picture even went up I actually got an email from "livenlove". His real name was Dave and he moved here four months ago from Vermont. Already I was in love just talking to him with that adorable New England accent. And the great thing was I actually got to talk on the phone (unlike Clive) and we had so much in common. He was from New England—I liked New England accents. He was new here—I was newly single. What else? Oh, it didn't matter because we were off to a great start. Plus he said he had been told before that he looked a little like Enrique Iglesias. I was loving this internet dating thing already. Enrique liked hot, sexy women so I would definitely wear my sexy, strappy sandals with my black, tight jeans and a sexy top. Problem was, my concept of sexy back then was something that came a little below my neckline and wasn't long sleeved. Anyway the big night came and I took extra care with my hair and makeup and was just about to leave when the thought occurred to me that while Enrique might like hot, sexy women, Dave might not. Back to the closet and out came my regular jeans and a top that came up to my neck and had full length sleeves. I left the strappy sandals on, just in case! We had agreed to meet for dinner at a nearby Indian place so it would be quiet and we could get to know each other better. Fortunately when I arrived there were only two families having dinner so it would be easy to spot my Enrique even if he didn't look exactly like him. Someone pulled up in a Honda Civic with Vermont license plates, and my heart starting pounding. And then there he was—my Enrique! Well, actually it was a shorter, stockier, balding version of Enrique. So the first words I blurted out when he said hello were "Who told you that you looked like Enrique?" It probably wasn't a good ice breaker, but I was pretty much in a worse state of shock than when I met Clive. Anyway Dave blushed and mumbled something about how he used to get told a lot how much he looked like the handsome Latin.

Dave: "I guess you don't think I resemble him much?"

Me: "I'm sorry. I mean you probably do look like Enrique, but I quit watching MTV years ago so I'm a little fuzzy about how he looks."

Dave: "No, it's cool. I just figured that when you saw my ad you would have been able to tell."

Me: "When I saw your ad?"

Dave: "Yeah, my ad on datesrgreats.com. You did read it and see my picture, right?"

Me: "Oh sure."

Anyway that was about the most stimulating that the conversation got all evening. But I learned two things from my not so great date:

1. Never agree to have dinner with a man that you've never met before. If you just have coffee or a drink, you're out of there in a half hour max and don't have to suffer through a one to two hour dinner (depending on how the service is that evening), and:

2. Always, always, always read the ads and look at the pictures before going out with someone. VERY IMPORTANT!!!

So I went home that evening fairly bummed. I had gone out with two promising men, both of whom were overweight and balding and unbelievable bores. Not that I'm such a great conversationalist, but at least I'm fairly attractive. Heroditus was greeting me at the door when I got home.

"At least you love me, don't you baby?" With Heroditus it was never clear if it was me or his Tasty Kritters canned food that he loved more. While Heroditus was indulging himself with Gizzard and Liver Pate, I decided to have a late night snack. I barely ate at the Indian restaurant because I was feeling pretty queasy after seeing Dave in his Honda Civic. There was one tiny problem with having a late night snack—I had no food in the refrigerator because I really hated cooking now that I lived alone. Ok, it's cool. I'll just go to bed hungry and bummed. The next tiny problem was that I was so wound up I couldn't sleep. I thought about the whole idea of cooking for one person and wondered how other people handled the situation. So I did the only logical thing when you're hungry and can't sleep—I went to the computer and wrote a little ditty:

Cooking For One

Prime rib, pork chops, roast turkey. Throw away those recipes! 'Cause I'm cooking for one now, yeah, cooking for one now. It's only me. I'm filled with glee. 'Cause I'm cooking for one now, yeah, cooking for one now. Potstickers, wontons, teriyaki. Vindaloo, naan, tandoori. I'm cooking for one now, yeah, cooking for one now. Won't ever need those pots and pans. Throw out the spices, starches and cans. 'Cause I'm cooking for one now, yeah, cooking for one now. Cobblers, cakes and Crepes Suzettes. Won't see me grilling thick fillets. Cause I'm cooking for one now, yeah, cooking for one now. Child, Pepin and Legasse. Find someone else, hey can't you see? I'm cooking for one now, yeah, cooking for one now. It's only me. Oh lucky me. I'm cooking for one now!

Maybe this is how McCartney and Lennon got started?! Probably not, but I did feel better after writing it and did eventually manage to fall asleep. The next morning I was hung over—not from alcohol but from unhappiness.

Dave was actually a nice guy and it wasn't his fault that he thought he looked like Enrique Iglesias. It had never occurred to me that if he looked like Enrique Iglesias, he most likely would not have needed the internet to find women. That thought made me even more unhappy. It took me back to my original concept that the internet was for losers. Just emblazon a big red "L" on my forehead to advertise my looserosity. Anyway, I kept thinking about how Dave had really been very polite and handled my faux pas about him not looking like Enrique in a sweet way. He was a total gentleman even when I think he knew that I arranged for the waiter to tell me the baby sitter called and my son was ill and I needed to go home immediately. One of the reasons I think he knew I was lying is when I reread my ad later that evening, I saw that I had put in it that I had no children. Another important lesson to be learned about online dating: always remember what you write in your ad so if you have to tell a little white lie it doesn't come back to bite you! All day long I kept thinking about how nice Dave was, and that he would treat me so well, and I could somehow learn to like him if I really tried, couldn't I?

"No, Cynthia." (that mysterious voice said).

"You could not learn to like him."

"But why?" (I asked the mystery voice)

"You're not attracted to him." (was the mystery voice reply)

"OK, M.V., but looks aren't everything, right?" "Looks aren't everything, right?"

"Mystery Voice, are you there?"

Why does the damn mystery voice always leave you when you most need advice?!

Anyway the next day I received an email from "nicegisfinish1st". He wrote me a five paragraph email that I managed to get through two paragraphs before responding back that I'd love to exchange phone numbers with him. There was no photo provided with his profile, but he was 5'10', black hair and green eyes. Sounds good on paper. And his screen name says he's a nice guy. So the following day, Carey (Mr. Nice Gi) called me and we talked briefly because I was running late for a hair appointment. We agreed to meet for coffee that Friday at Moondollars. Moondollars had the best double decaf mocha caramel butterscotch latte in the world, so even if Carey and I didn't hit it off, I could have a yummy latte and maybe a triple fudge white chocolate chip brownie. As usual, I arrived early and it was a little crowded, so I was concerned I couldn't spot him since I never actually saw his photo. My cell went off about ten minutes later, and it was Carey telling me to look over in the corner behind the magazine and newspaper rack. As I turned around, there he was waving at me from a table. Well at least he had hair and a nice smile, although Brad Pitt had nothing to worry about from this guy.

Carey: "Are you Cynthia?"
Me: "No, I'm Patricia. I think you're supposed to meet Cynthia here tomorrow night!"
Carey looked very puzzled and I laughed and told him I was joking.
Carey: "Oh, right."

There wasn't even the teensiest giggle at my joke. It was going to be a long latte drinking night.

Me: "So, Carey, I noticed in your profile that you're self employed. What exactly do you do?"
Carey: "I bake cookies."
Me: "Do you want to expand on that a bit?"

Carey spent the next 40 minutes and 32 seconds expanding. Seems he was trying to get a cookie baking business going but was having a rough time of it. His mother died when he was 13 and he and his older sister were basically alone. Apparently they lived in one slum hole after another. He had his first job at 16 and was now working two different jobs to raise enough money to do some marketing for his cookie business.

Me: "When do you have time to bake the cookies if you work two jobs?"

Carey: "I get up at 3 every morning and bake about 5 dozen different types of cookies and take them around to various grocery stores and local markets hoping to sell them."

Me: "So, how do you have time to date?"

Carey: "Oh, you're the first girl I've gone out with. You're actually the only girl who responded to my emails, and I was really excited to meet you."

Ok he scored some brownie points (or should I say "cookie points"?) for calling me a girl, but this poor guy had no money and probably not much of a future. Plus he was 35 and never been married. I grew up in the generation that if you weren't married by the time you were 30, there was definitely something wrong with you. It was an old fashioned mind set, I know, but I couldn't quite shake it. Anyway after an appropriate amount of time I thanked him for the latte (he didn't offer anything else so I never got my brownie) and told him I had to go. He insisted on walking me to my car and asked if I'd like to see him again. I thought I had made it obvious I didn't, but I guess he didn't take the hint well.

Me: "Let me think about it."

Carey: "Sure. Hey I want to give you some cookies to try."

Me: "Oh, that's so sweet, but I'm starting a diet tomorrow and…"

Carey: "You sure don't look like you need to lose any weight. You have a very nice figure, if you don't mind me saying something so forward."

No, I didn't mind at all! He just scored a few more points, but it would take a lot more than that to convince me to go out with him again. One thing I have to say for him is he was persistent because by the time I left the parking lot, I had in my possession a tiny foil wrapped box with a pretty pink and white striped bow and fresh white tea rose on top containing his cookies. I felt so guilty taking it because I knew he must have taken great care in wrapping it for me, and it was all wasted effort on his part. Two days later I received a call from Carey asking how I liked the cookies. OH NO!! I left them in the car and totally forgot about them.

Me: "Oh, they're wonderful!", I lied.
Carey: "Which one was your favorite?"

Shit! It never pays to lie! Most likely he would have had chocolate chip in there so I felt I was safe in telling him I liked the chocolate chip the best.

Carey: "I don't make chocolate chip. Everyone does them so I never do. You must be talking about the fudge coconut cookie. Maybe you mistook it for chocolate chip?"
Me: "Describe it to me."
Carey: "Well it's chocolate in color, of course, with bits of coconut and walnuts in it."
Me: "Oh yeah, how stupid of me to think it was chocolate chip. Duh!"
Carey: "Were there any others that you especially liked?"

I hadn't done well with lie number one, so I wasn't feeling very confident at this point about my fabricating skills.

Me: "Well you know how I told you I was starting my diet and all so I'm only allowing myself one cookie per day."
Carey: "Right. So what was the other cookie you had?"
Me: "Peanut butter."

No point in even thinking hard because I had a 50-50 chance of being right.

Carey: "It's not actually peanut butter. I have peanuts and butterscotch chips that I blend into a basic sugar cookie batter. Is that what you mean?"

Thank you, God, for making Carey so dense.

Me: "Yeah, it tastes just like peanut butter."
Carey: "That's odd. You're the first person who ever thought that."
Me: "Carey, I think I should tell you that I had a high fever when I was a kid and it affected my tongue, so my taste buds aren't what they should be exactly."

I was on a roll with the lies now and it felt pretty good.
Carey: "I'm so sorry. That must be horrible for you to confuse food all of the time."
Me: "Well, it's not so bad. I take medication for it."
Carey: "Oh. What type of medication do you take?"
Me: "It has a really long name that you probably never heard of and I take the generic brand because it's cheaper, of course."
Carey: "They have generic meds for tongue problems?"
Me: "Yes. What marvelous advances the medical industry has made in the last few years, huh?"

Carey: "Yeah! I think I'll look it up in the internet. I've never heard of such a thing. Here I am going out with a girl who has a taste bud disease, and I know nothing about the disease."

There were two things that really upset me about his last comment. One, that he was going to look up my non-existent taste bud disease on the internet; and, two, that he referred to me as the "girl he was going out with." There was only one thing to do, and that was to ignore his comment and pretend that someone was at the door and I had to go.

Carey: "I didn't hear the doorbell."
Me: "It's got a silent ringer. It just sort of vibrates, you know?"
Carey: "Really? And you can feel the vibration?"
Me: "Yes, it's very powerful. I can actually feel it within about a 25 foot radius."
Carey: "Very weird! Well, when can we see each other again?"

The dreaded question!!!

Me: "I've got a really hectic week ahead so let me get back to you, ok?"
Carey: "Sure, sounds great, Cynthia."

I should have just told him right then and there that I wasn't interested, but I was feeling really guilty for leaving his cookies in the car, lying about eating them and pretending to have a taste bud disease. (I had already forgotten about the silent, vibrating doorbell lie). The least I could do before breaking his heart was to eat one of his cookies, which were probably unbelievably stale by now. So off I went to my car to retrieve his beautifully wrapped package with the now wilted flower. Normally I had dessert after dinner, but it was just one cookie. I picked one out that looked like it was not the two we had already discussed so I could actually be honest about the cookie I ate next time we talked. I bit into the cookie and started chewing it when something extraordinary occurred. There was a strong urge to get down on my knees and thank God that I really didn't have a taste bud disease because no human should go through life without tasting this exquisite cookie. Too bad I had lied about eating them because I wanted to rush to the phone and tell him what a genius he was! The cookie was vanilla flavored with tiny pieces of peppermint laced through it. Peppermint was not one of my favorites but it just seemed married to the vanilla in a way I could never begin to explain. Maybe this was his specialty, and I should try another just to see. The next cookie I tried was chocolate with swirls of caramel throughout. Sublime! I really felt I needed to try one more and that was going to be it, or I'd never eat dinner. It was a mocha almond fudge sensation! With each bite of each cookie, I came closer to paradise or nirvana or heaven or wherever it was we were headed for. (With all of the lies I was telling I probably was headed in the opposite direction!). I wasn't much for organized religion, and the last time I "saw" the inside of a church was when I was baptized at age two. But these cookies were created by God Himself! They had to be. So I had found God on the internet disguised as Carey Nicegisfinish1st. Who would have guessed? Needless to say, I never did have dinner that night, but I did eat one dozen of the most awesome cookies ever created. And they were two days old! The next time I talked to Carey, which was the following day, I had to tell him that I didn't feel we had much in common. I did praise him to no end for his magnificent cookies and wished him nothing but luck and happiness in his life. It was all done very tastefully and in the kindest, gentlest manner possible. Actually I left the message on his answering machine during the time I knew he was working.

What a coward I am! The following week he called me and was chatting as though he never received my message.

Me: "Didn't you get my message?"

Carey: "No. You left me a message?", he asked obviously overjoyed that I had called him. "My answering machine hasn't been working for over a week, and I haven't had time to take it in to be fixed."

Fuck a duck!!! I didn't have the heart to tell him over the phone so I agreed to see him and thought I could tell him when we met at Moondollars. How wrong was I! It's even more difficult to tell someone when you see them face to face.

Me: "So, when do you think you'll be getting your answering machine fixed?"

Carey: "Probably not for another couple of weeks because I got a job from some high society lady in Newport Beach to make 30 dozen cookies for her daughter's 10th birthday party, and I'm trying out some new recipes. I'm really feeling that this is going to be the big break I've been waiting for."

Me: "Fantastic news!!! Hey, I'm going to the electronic shop tomorrow, and I wouldn't mind taking the machine in for you, if you like."

Carey: "You are the nicest person I've ever met. But I couldn't put you out like that."

You poor, dense ignoramus! I'm doing it so I can leave you a "Dear Carey" message because I'm too much of a weenie to do it in person. I didn't actually say this to him, of course. What I did say was…..

Me: "It's no trouble at all, really."

Carey: "Ok. But only if you let me buy you lunch."

Me: (smiling through my teeth) "Oh that would be great."

Carey: "Hey, I almost forgot—I brought you a little present."

He started fumbling around but couldn't find what he was looking for. My only thought was please don't let it be jewelry—that just screams commitment!

Carey: "I must have left it at home. Darn!!! Can I give it to you tomorrow at lunch?"

Me: (more smiling through my teeth) "That's cool, but you really shouldn't, you know."

Carey: "You're one of the sweetest, prettiest girls I've ever met and I really should."

Well I had no response to that. My thought was since he was so busy baking cookies he didn't know anyone else, but that didn't sit well with me because I wanted to truly be one of the sweetest, prettiest girls (love the "girls" bit).

So the following day I had lunch with him at some second rate coffee shop which I knew he could barely afford. My "present" was another beautifully wrapped box of cookies. Great! Just what I need when I'm trying to look good for all these potential hunks I'll be meeting. Hopefully, his answering machine would be fixed soon, and I could put an end to what I didn't seem able to put an end to in person. Lunch was pretty dreadful, and he apologized for being so quiet.

Carey: "I was up until 4:30 this morning baking, so only got a couple hours sleep. My boss at my day job wanted me to work OT so that leaves me no time later today to do my shopping for some new cookie recipes I have ideas for. Everything has to be perfect for this Newport Beach birthday party."

Me: "Why didn't you say something? We could have so cancelled today." (He had no idea how we could have so cancelled today)

Carey: "Are you serious? I'd never want to give up an opportunity to see you. I know you are really busy also, so I try to adjust my schedule to see you whenever you have the time."

Guilt was setting in.

Carey: "I'm really hoping that if this woman in Newport Beach spreads the word that my career will start taking off, and I can quit at least one of my jobs. Then I can be move available to see you more often."

More guilt was setting in.

Carey: "Are you a little shy? I feel that you are really holding back, but I'm not sure why."

Guilt is rising to a boiling point now.

Me: "Carey, you're really a nice, nice person. I mean you really are. But I just don't feel what I think I should feel, you know?"

He looked at me quizzically. Uh oh---he didn't know!

Me: "You deserve someone really special. Right now I'm just not looking for any kind of commitment. I want to date around, you know?"

Again the puzzled look from him.

Carey: "I don't mind if you see other guys, Cynthia. I know we just met and it takes time to develop really strong feelings."

Shit! How do you break up with someone that you're not even going out with? I went back to work feeling miserable and pondering how in the hell I was going to get the message across to this guy that I wasn't interested. I opened up his box of cookies and, of course, ate the whole freaking box even though I just had lunch. He may not be the best looking nor wealthiest guy in the world, but damn he could bake a mean cookie! Driving home from work was pure hell because it had rained, and anytime two raindrops fall in Southern California drivers act as though they have never driven in rain. As I sat in the inevitable bumper to bumper, I pondered what to do about my "relationship" with Carey. Then Mysterious Voice appeared:

M.V.: "Why are you still wasting this guy's time?"
Me: "I give up, you tell me."
M.V.: "He's really holding you back from meeting someone you might truly care for."
Me: "Not true! So not true! I'm free to date other guys, didn't you hear him tell me that?"
M.V.: "Right! So why aren't you?"
Me: "Huh?"
M.V.: "You heard me. You're just wasting your time and his, and he's too nice of a guy."
Me: "He's too nice of a guy to waste his time, or he's too nice of a guy for me?"

As usual mysterious voice flaked on me so I wasn't sure what he was too nice of a guy for. I was also annoyed that I continually had a problem communicating with him. Was he really that dense that he couldn't tell how I felt? Maybe he was just lonely and would settle for anyone? Well, that wasn't very flattering to me. Anyway it was now over a month, and I still hadn't the courage to just tell him I didn't want to see him anymore—partly because I was a coward and partly because I adored those damn cookies of his! That night after eating my Weight Watchers frozen entrée (which allowed me to eat ½ box of Carey's cookies if I cheated just a little bit), I sat down to watch television (something I rarely do) and grabbed Heroditus up on my lap. He immediately jumped down which was something he rarely did. Oh God even my cat thinks I'm horrible for the way I'm treating Carey! Or maybe he's pissed that I'm not sharing the cookies with him? I picked up the phone and dialed his number. Of course the answering machine clicked on, and I told him what I could not bring myself to do so many times before. I don't remember my exact words, but they were something to the effect that I felt it was best if we didn't see each other again because he deserved only the best and I had no feelings for him etc. etc. The next morning I received the following email from him:

"Cynthia, I've known all along that you didn't have the feelings for me that I had for you. I really hoped that in time you would come around. But I respect you for being honest with me, and I wish you all the best in the world."

So that was it. He respected me for being honest! The only time I had truly been honest with him was when I told him how much I loved his cookies. Of course, Mysterious Voice had to put her two cents in.

M.V.: "Well don't you feel better now?"

Me: "Yeah, I guess. But he was such a nice guy, and I don't get why I couldn't be attracted to him. And the cookies! The cookies, Mysterious Voice!!"

M.V.: "Well I don't know anything about the cookies

because you never shared, but you weren't attracted to him because he <u>was</u> such a nice guy."

Me: "That is so not true! If I had been attracted to him I would have loved the fact that he was such a nice guy. I would have loved it!"

M.V.: "Why do you think guys are nice? Because they have to be!! Women want someone who is: 1.Wealthy and will take care of them; or 2. Attractive; or preferably 3. Wealthy and attractive. Guys who are none of the above have to compensate in some way so they become obnoxiously nice hoping they can win you over."

Me: "You are so fucking shallow, and that is absolutely not true. Just leave me alone! Just fucking leave me alone!"

M.V.: "You said fuck twice."

Me: "What?!"

M.V.: "You said fuck twice. I told you before not to use the "f" word with me."

Me: "I can't even believe I'm having this conversation with you."

A very long pause ensued.

Me: "You left again, didn't you? Fine, just don't come back because your input is faulty and nonsensical and fucked up! OOOH I said it again!"

UNCLE NATHAN

My internet dating was going quite well once Carey was out of the picture, and I was seeing at least one person a week— sometimes several per week. One night my mother called and asked if I'd like to have lunch the next day. That meant only one thing—she needed a favor. Since I wasn't much of a cook (peanut butter and jelly sandwiches were my specialty) and Mother was an excellent one, I always looked forward to sampling her goodies even if it involved something from me in return. Actually, I'm not much of a housekeeper either— no wonder Sebastian left me for another! Anyway, I had no problem with doing Mother a favor as long as it didn't involve Uncle Nathan. Uncle Nathan was my mother's great uncle who had lived with her when she was growing up. My guess is he was now about 125 years old and talk about crotchety!!! Generally I would time my visits with my mother when Uncle Nathan was napping (which was roughly every three to four hours) or out with his friends playing bingo. It was hard to believe Uncle Nathan had any friends—not only because of his age but also because of his disposition. When I arrived at Mother's I could smell pungent barbecue sauce coming from the kitchen. Not exactly my favorite, but that was a good sign—it meant Mother was not going to ask me for an Uncle Nathan related favor. She normally made Coquilles St. Jacques when it involved Uncle Nathan because she knew it was my favorite, even if it was a pretty retro recipe.

Me: "What'cha cooking?"
Mother: "Your favorite! It's all ready for you on the table."

Oh shit! Not only had she made Coquille St. Jacques, but she put the scallops on her beautiful white ivory scallop platter. This meant a major favor and Uncle Nathan definitely was involved.

Me: "How come I smell barbecue sauce?"
Mother: "I'm making barbecue pork for dinner tonight."
Me: "Aren't you going to a lot of trouble with all this cooking?"

Mother didn't say anything, but turned her back to me and pretended like she was looking for something in the cabinet.

Me: "I thought Uncle Nathan hated pork."

Mother: "No, he likes it but when he converted to the Moslem religion he quit eating it."

Me: "Yeah, but then he converted to Jehovah Witness after that. They eat pork, don't they?"

Mother: "Yes, but then he converted to Judaism and even though he was reformed, he felt he shouldn't eat pork."

Me: "When did he do that? I didn't even know."

Mother: "Last year, but now he's back to being an atheist."

Me: "So why won't he eat pork?"

Mother: "You don't want to know."

Me: "So why are you going to so much trouble if only you eat the pork?"

Again mother turned her back and pretended to be looking for something.

Me: "Mother, do you have some hot stud muffin coming over tonight?"

I was joking, of course, because mother had not had a date since she and my dad divorced, and that was when I was 18. My father had decided that he preferred 25 year old blondes with skinny bodies and big boobs to his 40something, graying, wrinkled, bulging, saggy breasted wife. Apparently divorce to my father meant divorcing everything that went with the marriage so my older sister, Sara, and I also were out of his life before the ink on the divorce paper was dry. He moved back to New York state and the last we heard (from nosey relatives) he was still boning the young, beautiful blondes. Anyway back to my mother and my facetious comment. It turns out that she had actually met someone at a flea market, and they went out once or twice and he was now coming for dinner tonight. For obvious reasons, she did not want Uncle Nathan in the house when he came. My mother had probably not had sex in many moons, and I wondered what had happened to make her suddenly get interested in it again. I was so thrilled for her that I even happily consented to take Uncle Nathan out for the evening.

Me: "Mother, did you want Uncle Nathan to spend the night with me?"

I asked this very apprehensively.

Mother: "No of course not. Peter is just coming for dinner and should be gone by about 8."
Me: "Wow he works fast!"
Mother: "What do you mean?"
Me: "Well if he can have dinner and dessert by 8, he's a fast mover."

My mother didn't get my obvious dessert reference so I left it at that. It was a generation gap thing. If I invited a guy for dinner it was just understood that I was inviting him for more than just filet mignon! It never occurred to me that mother might just want a man for companionship and nothing more would come of it. I sincerely hoped that I never got to that point in my life where I looked at a man as a companion only, when they had so much more to offer! Anyway I had one appointment in between now and Uncle Nathan time so I hugged Mother goodbye and was off. Normally spending any time with Uncle Nathan was a horror, but I was ok with it today. I truly was excited for my mother to have found someone and also was even more excited about Brian, my date for tomorrow evening. He was ten years younger than me, very good looking (judging from his internet picture) and was a stockbroker. We also had some great phone conversations, so I knew it was going to be a fun evening.

Mysterious Voice: "You're going out with someone ten years younger than you?"

Me: "What's the big deal? Guys have been doing it for years. This is a whole new world, M.V. Get with it!"

Mysterious Voice: "Yes, but you weren't brought up in this whole new world, and the whole old world says he's too young for you."

Me: "Lots of women have younger men now. Look at Madonna and Cher and Demi Moore."

Mysterious Voice: "Yeah, but you're not exactly Madonna, Cher or Demi Moore!"

Me: "Big fucking deal! Maybe I'm not a glamorous star nor wealthy but I look pretty good for my age and most people are stunned when they hear that I'm the age I am. I have Madonna for my role model and she's done ok for herself."

As usual Mysterious Voice was gone. She was probably annoyed that I used the "F" word again. Anyway I considered myself a pioneer for the common woman in the field of dating a man regardless of his age. Someday young women would read about me in the history books and say "Thank God for Cynthia Mills. She broke down the barriers of age in dating." My fantasizing came to an abrupt end because I had arrived at my appointment. As I was leaving the appointment on the way to pick up good old Uncle Nathan, I received a call from Greg who asked me out for Saturday. Wow! The weekend was shaping up nicely for me. I could certainly endure a couple of hours of Uncle Nathan. When I walked in the house Uncle Nathan was waiting for me.

Me: "Hey, Uncle Nathan, your date is right on time!"

Uncle Nathan just sneered and followed me to my silver Jaguar. Sebastian had agreed to give me the car as part of our divorce agreement, probably because Daryl (Yep, still sublimating) was allergic to the car's leather upholstery. Fortunately Uncle Nathan was not in a chatty mood so we drove in silence to the restaurant. I chose the Meatball Market for dinner because it was fairly close to the house and would not be too busy this early in the evening. Once we were seated Uncle Nathan was the first to talk.

Uncle Nathan: "So your husband dumped you."
Me: "We mutually decided to end the marriage."
Uncle Nathan: "Tshhh."

He did that a lot and it was really annoying. Half way through dinner Uncle Nathan started making a fuss that he wanted a different table. The manager agreed to seat us in the next section and three waiters had to come to help us transport our half-eaten meals to our new spot. I knew the reason Uncle Nathan wanted to move. We had a male waiter at our first table, and there was a young, busty waitress handling the section we moved to. This was pretty scary, but I knew it was best to not get Uncle Nathan too worked up and have things really get ugly. The last time Uncle Nathan wanted to sit where the pretty waitress was we ended up at the police station for three hours because he grabbed her boobs when she was serving his entrée to him.

Me: "If you even so much as lift your hand toward this woman's body, I'm leaving and you can pay the bill yourself and walk home!"

I felt somewhat secure that this would work because Uncle Nathan was the cheapest bastard to ever walk the face of the earth, and as far as he was concerned no woman's breast was worth paying for dinner. As we waited for the check, Uncle Nathan yelled at the top of his voice that he had just peed in his pants.

Me: "You're hysterical, Uncle Nathan! Are you enjoying making an ass out of yourself in front of everyone? Don't think for a minute that you're embarrassing me, old coot."

This wasn't the first time he had done this and most likely would not be the last. But it always had a great shock effect on everyone that heard him. On the way home, my dear uncle once again brought up the subject of my divorce.

Uncle Nathan: "You still married to that geek?"

I ignored him.

Uncle Nathan: "He dumped you, didn't he? The geek dumped you. Tshhh."

When we got to mother's home, no car was in the drive so I figured it was safe to just drop Uncle Nathan off and go home. I called mother from my cell and she told me her dinner was wonderful and waived as she opened the door for good old Uncle Nathan.

The next morning I was up very early in order to get several appointments in before noon because I was meeting an old college roommate for lunch and then that evening was my big date with Brian. I had to stop at the drug store first to pick up a few sundries. While I was there, I noticed the most gorgeous hunkster staring at me. We both smiled and as he approached me he started singing "Younger Than Springtime" from South Pacific. Figures, the good looking ones are either gay, married or psychopaths.

Good Looking Psychopath: "Gayer than laughter, am I. Softer than---"

Just then a woman in the next aisle walked toward me with a bottle of shampoo in her hands.

Woman in next aisle: "I'm gonna wash that man right outa my hair, I'm gonna wash that man right outa my hair and send him on his way. Get the picture?"

Apparently all of the women in the store except me did get the picture because they all started following her singing the chorus. Was I in the middle of a very bizarre dream? I started looking around for a hidden camera. Maybe it was some new show that was secretly being filmed to show how normal people react to weird situations. The cashier by this time had also joined the South Pacific processional trying to wash their men out of their hair! Suddenly I gasped as a masked gunman was helping himself to the money in the cash register. He looked up and saw me and started walking toward me. Oh my God, he's going to kill me right in the middle of this out of body experience I was having. When he got right up to me he started singing the Jet song.

Masked gunman: "When you're a Jet little world step aside, let them go underground, let them run let them hide."

As if all of this wasn't unreal enough, Heroditus suddenly appeared. I tried to grab him but he let out a shriek and jumped off the bed. Wait a minute the bed? Good lord I was dreaming this. Of all the strange dreams, this was by far the strangest. It must have been my evening with Uncle Nathan. He'd bring out bizarro behavior in anyone. Anyway I climbed out of bed trying to shake the dream out of my head and get ready for my luncheon with my pal, Nikki. Nikki—legal name Nicolette Hughes McLaren Mohammed Jankowski soon-to-be Ranier (no relation to the Monaco Raniers) was late for our luncheon engagement as she normally was. Then suddenly---

Nikki: "Hey, dudette!" she yelled this from the other side of the room. One thing about Nikki—she always knew how to attract attention.

Me: "Hey!"

We're off to a stimulating conversation. Nikki was a wedding coordinator who was obviously quite good at what she did since she had planned her own wedding so many times. She had already told me on the phone the day before that if husband number four did not work out, she was not walking down anymore aisles. We both pretty much knew that was a lie. Nikki was giving Liz Taylor a real run for her money! I decided to break the ice by telling her my weird dream. Never one to be outdone, she told me a dream she had where she was naked (of course) and standing at the edge of Niagara Falls reciting the Declaration of Independence.

Me: "So how are the wedding plans coming?"
Nikki: "I have two weeks to convince Charles (she pronounced it 'Sharl', like the French say it) to let me go to the Shangri La Spa so I can fit in to my gown by the time the wedding takes place."
Me: "Let me guess, you're wearing a white wedding gown?"
Nikki: "Absolutement madame! It's breathtaking and has a four foot train."
Me: "How many bridesmaids this time?"
Nikki: "Only five. You know I would have loved to have you in my wedding, sugar plum, but since you were in the last one I just felt it would be bad luck."
Me: "Not a problem."

Another thing about Nikki is that she manages to stay

friends with all the friends of her former husbands, so she has a whole pisspot full of bridesmaids to choose from.

Nikki: "I always wanted a rainbow wedding, so that's what we're having. Charles is such a lambie pie about letting me do what I want."

Me: "Uh huh."

Nikki: "Actually I feel a little guilty because this is his first marriage and he's pretty much given me complete control in planning it."

Me: "Uh huh."

Nikki: "I think he feels since I'm in the business there's no point in him toying with the expert."

Me: "Uh huh."

Nikki: "I ordered most of the flowers from a honey love I met in Hawaii when I was on my last honeymoon. He does the most extraordinary arrangements and I told him the next time I got married I would die if I couldn't have him for the florist. Little did I know there actually would be a next time."

Me: "Uh huh."

Nikki: "Oh no more about me, sweet potato, tell me all about your internet dating. I've never tried that before but I bet you meet tons of guys."

Me: "Nikki, I honestly don't think you need it."

Nikki: "God, I hope Charles doesn't want a church wedding. He doesn't even know I'm a semi-atheist."

So much for her talking about me!

Me: "What's a semi-atheist?"

Nikki: "Well it's where one day you think there's a God and then the next day no way."

Me: "Isn't that kind of what an agnostic is?"

I prided myself on being a member of the latter group. Atheist just sounds too harsh.

Just then, my cell phone went off (I had forgotten to shut it off which I normally do when I'm having a meal-bad for the digestion, you know). It was my mother on the phone and she was in a slight panic. She wanted me to go with her to pick up Uncle Nathan. Seems he and his buddies went on a joyride and ended up getting rear ended. Everyone was fine but the car was smashed in and had to be towed. It was amazing to me that any of those 100somethings were still allowed to drive.

Me: "Mother, are you afraid to drive during the day now also?"

Mother had been a little uneasy about driving at night lately.

Mother: "No, I just don't like driving long distances."
Me: "Long distances?"
Mother: "Well I guess I forgot to mention that Uncle Nathan is in Hollywood."
Me: "Yeah, you actually did forget that tiny detail. I'm half afraid to ask why Uncle Nathan is in Hollywood."
Mother: "Um, I think he was sort of on his way to a porn shop."
Me: "Why Hollywood?! Don't they have porn shops in Orange County?"
Mother: "This is some special shop. Oh I don't even want to discuss it right now. It's best that you don't ask."

So I had to cut short my lunch with Nikki to go get Uncle Nathan. I had hoped since it was only 1:30 that we wouldn't hit much traffic. And if there hadn't been three accidents on the freeway that afternoon, we might have made good time. It was almost 5 p.m. by the time we arrived at Sunset Boulevard. My date with Brian was supposed to be at 7. Wow it was going to be tight but at least we could ride in the carpool most of the way. When Uncle Nathan got in the car, the first words out of his mouth were to ask if we could still stop at Whips And Lashes (evidently the shop he never made it to).

Me: "Don't you think you owe us an apology for driving all this way rather than inconveniencing us even more?"

Uncle Nathan: "Tshh."

Me: "You know, I absolutely hate when you make that stupid sound! I have a date in less than two hours and you better start praying, pal, that there's no traffic on the way home."

Mother: "Is that one of your internet dates?"

Great! I knew what was coming next--my mother lecturing me about going out with strange men etc. etc. I was not in the mood for lectures because we were now on the freeway and even the carpool lane was moving at a snails pace.

Me: "Yeah, why?"

I was getting defensive already.

Mother: "There are plenty of nice men that you could meet in a more normal setting than finding some who knows what on the computer."

Me: "Really? Well why don't you tell me where all these nice men are hanging out, Mother, because I don't seem to be running into them as easily as you obviously are!"

I was treading on dangerous water and I knew it, but I didn't care. The slow moving traffic was really starting to annoy me. Uncle Nathan's stupid antics were annoying me.

My mother interfering with my life was annoying me. And the sudden realization that I forgot to bring Brian's number with me was annoying me even more!

Mother: "What about grocery stores or church or---"
Me: "Church? You and I haven't been inside a church for a million years so tell me how I'm supposed to meet someone at church?"

My voice was starting to get pretty loud, but again I didn't care.

Mother: "Well one of my bridge ladies goes regularly and she has met some very nice young men."
Me: "Your friend's concept of young and mine might be a little different!"

As soon as the words came out of my mouth, I knew I shouldn't have said it. Now we were on to her next favorite topic to annoy me with—me going out with younger men.

Mother: "How old is this internet person?"

She said the words 'internet person' as though she had just swallowed a turd.

Me: "I don't remember and frankly who gives a shit!"
Mother: "Well what if he wants to have children. How are you going to explain to him that your childbearing years are pretty much over? What then?"

We were both pretty much shouting at each other at this point, and Uncle Nathan was sitting quietly in the back seat loving every minute of our increasingly verbal quarrel.

Me: "What planet are you living on, Mother? I'm going out on my FIRST DATE with this guy. We won't be discussing my child bearing capabilities, believe me. And for your information, I am most capable of still bearing children."

Mother: "When your child is fifty, you'll be in your 90's. What kind of a mother can you be with that kind of age difference?"

Me: "I don't believe the fucking bullshit that you're coming up with!"

Mother: "Sshh. I don't think Uncle Nathan should hear you say that word."

I looked incredulously at her.

Me: "I'd just like to remind you that the reason we are sitting in bumper to bumper traffic right now, and I'm most likely going to miss my date with the man who according to you won't want to see me anyway because of my questionable child bearing capabilities is because Uncle Nathan was on his way to a pornographic shop to do who know's what, so I really don't think his hearing me say "fuck" is going to shock him too much!"

Uncle Nathan: "Tshh."

Me: "Old man you do that one more time and I swear I'm throwing you out of the car and you can walk home. And, oh yeah, why did you have to go all the way to Hollywood to a porn shop? Our Orange County porn shops aren't good enough for you?"

Uncle Nathan: "They were having a 99 cent sale on Popeye The Pecker Man comic books."

I looked at my mother.

Mother: "I told you not to ask!"

The rest of the trip home was in silence. My throat was completely hoarse from yelling so much, and I was trying to figure out how I was going to explain all of this to Brian. We arrived home at exactly 7:15, but by the time I would have made myself presentable and drove to Newport Beach (we were meeting at Humble Harry's for a drink) it would have been 8:30. I fumbled around looking for his number and couldn't find it. There was, however, a bunch of crumbled up paper on the floor that Heroditus had obviously been entertaining himself with. Most likely Brian's phone number was in that crumbled mess. I decided to at least email him and apologize, apologize, apologize. Once I emailed him with an explanation (leaving out the porn shop stuff), I decided to call Nikki to apologize for leaving lunch so abruptly and also sort of cry on her shoulder about my screwed up day. She answered on the first ring and sounded vary harried.

Nikki: "Oh my God, sweet pea, I'm in a real quandary. Charles decided he wants to have a church wedding so I really have to scramble to get an annulment."

Me: "You can get married if you just have one annulment?"

Nikki: "No, honeysuckle, all three! Do you see the problem I have?

Me: "Yeah, Nikki, I don't think the Catholic Church will be thrilled about knowing you have been married three times before. I mean I don't think you can do three annulments."

Nikki: "Why? Oh, pumpkin seed, they have to let me! One of my dearest friends plays golf with the archbishop and I'm trying to see if he can pull some strings for me. Charles really wants a church wedding."

Me: "I thought you said Charles was leaving all the details up to you?"

Nikki: "Yes, but he just assumed we were doing a church wedding thing, you know?"

Me: "You never discussed this with him?"

Nikki: "No, should I have?"

Me: "I'm not even going to dignify that with an answer. Nikki, I have to be honest here. I'm not exactly an expert on religion, but I think you'll have a real problem getting the church to go along with three annulments."

Nikki: "Oh my God! What am I going to do? He's the love of my life—it's for real this time, I swear! I may have said that with the other three (she did in fact say almost the exact same words about the other three), but this time I feel in my heart it's forever."

(She had also felt in her heart that the last three would be forever, but it didn't seem like an appropriate time to bring that up.)

Her cell started ringing so she had to go. So much for me crying on someone's shoulder! Normally I would never go out to a bar alone, but I really needed it at this point. I stopped in Clancy's and found a table in the darkest part of the bar. No sooner had I sat down than some rather attractive guy approached me. Hey, maybe my mother was right about meeting someone in a more traditional setting. (Although bars probably weren't on her acceptable list either).

Rather Attractive Guy: "Hi, I'm Fred."

Me: "Cynthia. Good meeting you."

Fred: "I eat fire."

Me: "Really?!"

Back to internet dating for this baby! Anyway my new found friend, Fred, was a magician and I was treated to about four of his pretty lame magic tricks before I managed to escape (not before promising to come to his next show at the Magician's Castle in Santa Ana where I could actually see him eat fire). Had this been the day from hell or what?!! I made a mental note to send a very special thank you card to Uncle Nathan for screwing up my day royally.

DON'T ASK AND DEFINITELY DON'T TELL

The following morning I woke up feeling pretty bummed but cheered up immediately when I saw that Brian had answered my email and he was quite understanding about the previous night. Unfortunately, he was leaving on a business trip and wouldn't return until the following week, but promised to call when he got back. None of my other emails were especially enticing, so I sent the usual "thanks but no thanks" response to them and was just getting in to the shower when the phone rang. It was my mother (calling to apologize, no doubt). Wrong! She was calling to tell me one of her bridge ladies met a very nice guy at church and he was my age and she thought we'd really hit it off. Mother was offering me an olive branch, so I decided to take it. The guy's name was Gene and he was 41 and a widow with no kids. So far, so good! Mother didn't have any more details but suggested I come to her bridge game the following evening, and I could talk to Sally O'Connor, her bridge lady, about him. I told her I'd think about it. Spending an evening with mother's bridge ladies wasn't really high on my list of exciting things to do. Ever since Sebastian and I split, I felt her bridge ladies looked at me as though I had driven my husband into homosexuality (as if I could), but since nothing much was going on I considered it a possibility. When I arrived home that evening I checked emails and once again no one interesting on the agenda, so I had to break some more guys' hearts by blowing them off. Looks like it would be bridge at mother's tomorrow evening. One of the nice things about my mother's bridge nights was she always made something highly tasty so at least I'd have a nice feast instead of my usual scrambled egg whites on whole wheat toast. When I arrived they were already playing and Uncle Nathan was watching television in the den.

A curvaceous blonde was on Entertainment Tonight and Uncle Nathan jumped up from his chair and wiggled and shouted out "Va Va Voom!".

Me: "Shouldn't someone tell him that went out in the 50's?"
Mother: "What went out in the 50's?"
Me: "Va Va Voom!"
Mother: "I'm so accustomed to his idiosyncrasies that I don't even notice him anymore."
Me: "That's one good way to peacefully cohabit."
Mother: "I'm going to be serving refreshments soon so that would be a good time to talk to Mrs. O'Connor."
Me: "What are we having?"
Mother: "Braided Artichoke Bread, Hot Jalapeno Cheese Dip and Pineapple Upside Down Custard Cake."

Hmmm. Interesting combination, but again it beats scrambled egg whites on whole wheat toast. I munched on some Reeses Pieces that I found in the cupboard while I waited for the girls to finish their game. It seemed to be taking them longer than usual so I decided to go to the powder room to freshen up. There was a large bowl in the bathroom with the name M. Rimaldi taped to it and what appeared to be a dead goldfish inside the bowl. I wondered why Mrs. Rimaldi would bring a dead goldfish to our house. Anyway the bridge game was winding down when I returned so I asked Mrs. Rimaldi if that was her goldfish in the bathroom. A stupid question since her name was on the bowl, right? She acknowledged that it was and asked why I was asking.

Me: "Well the fish looked like it was dead and I…"

Mrs. Rimaldi let out an earpiercing scream and collapsed into the nearest chair. Everyone began running over to her and trying to calm her down. Mrs. Rimaldi was crying uncontrollably and just kept saying over and over: "Oh my God, Chloe!". Apparently Chloe was the name of her goldfish, and apparently she had what I considered to be an unnatural attachment to it. My mother told Mrs. Rimaldi that she would make her some tea and glared at me as she passed by. Mrs. Johnston felt it would be better if she had a straight shot of whiskey but Mrs. Rimaldi managed to compose herself for two seconds and waved her hand to dismiss that idea. Then Madge Thomasen told us about her brother-in-law, Harold, who went on a three week drinking binge when his goat died and ended up dying of liver damage shortly after that. Everyone, even me, thought that was in bad taste to upset poor Mrs. Rimaldi even more than she already was. Evie Hanover told Mrs. Rimaldi that Chloe had been very lucky to have such a wonderful owner like her. Donna Samuelson echoed that sentiment and told her that Chloe was probably already in goldfish heaven watching over Mrs. Rimaldi. From Anne Mausman:

"She was such a wonderful goldfish, and I know it's going to be hard for you. But you're a real trooper and you'll pull through this."

Mrs. O'Connor agreed and added:

"We don't always like the cards we're dealt in life, but you know we're all here for you, Mavis."

Me: "I didn't know your first name was Mavis!"

I was thinking that those two names didn't really go well together, but my thoughts were interrupted by the uncomfortable realization that the bridge women were looking at me strangely. I've never been very good at this stuff, but I decided that I needed to utter some words of comfort also.

Me: "You know, Mrs. Rimaldi, you can always get another goldfish."

My mother was just coming in with the tea when I said this and she gave me one of her "you cold, insensitive bitch" looks. As I said, I've never been good at this sort of comforting stuff mainly because I've never had anyone close to me pass away. Of course, we could count my father who was dead to me as far as I was concerned. Anyway, it seemed like every comforting death cliché had pretty much already been said so I decided to go to the kitchen for more Reeses Pieces since it was obvious this latest turn of events would delay the appetizers and dessert being served. My mother followed me in and didn't say a word, probably because she wanted me to meet this dude, Gene, and didn't want to start another argument at this time of great tragedy!

Mother: "Sally said there's a spaghetti dinner tomorrow evening at the church hall and Gene is going to be helping out with it. She and I thought it would be a great time for you to check him out and that way if you're not interested nothing needs to be said."

I agreed to do this for three reasons:

1. It would be the second night in a row that I would not have to eat scrambled egg whites on whole wheat toast.
2. I knew Mother would not be lecturing me about my dating because she would rather slaughter her first born child than let her friends know her daughter was seeing men from the internet, and
3. I don't remember what number three was, but there definitely was a number three.

Me: "What church is this anyway?"

Mother: "I think it's called the Evangelical Holisitic United Brethren Church."

Me: "There's a mouthful!"

For the second day in a row, my life had been disrupted by unexpected bizarre happenings. Unfortunately when I got home there were once again no promising emails.

I had pretty low expectations of anything coming of this Gene thing, so I didn't go to any great trouble to make myself look too gorgeous. My mother, Sally O'Connor and I had just begun eating our salads when Mrs. Rimaldi and Mrs. Tucker (another friend of my mother's who only subbed at bridge) came in. Mrs. Rimaldi was dressed from head to toe in black with a yellow ribbon pinned to her black vest. I asked my mother what the yellow ribbon was for and she replied that Mrs Rimaldi vowed to wear it every day because it was the same color as Chloe.

Me: "Have they announced when and where the funeral services are? Did Chloe have any particular flower that she was especially fond of that I could send?"

Mother just gave me one of her extra dirty looks and turned away to talk to Sally O'Connor. Hopefully Gene had a better sense of humor than her! I was munching one of the garlic sticks when my mother nudged her elbow into my ribs to announce that Sally O'Connor had just spotted Gene.

"Where is he?", I asked.

Mother motioned with her head to the opposite side of the room. Mrs. O'Connor was waving wildly to get his attention. He finally saw her and started walking over to our table. If he was forty, then I am twenty-nine! He had a butch haircut, wore glasses and was a little overweight. Not exactly my dream boy. Mrs. O'Connor was slobbering all over him with compliments when he finally arrived at our table, and my mother sort of kicked her under the table to remind her what she was supposed to do. She finally took the hint and started introducing two of "her dearest friends" to Gene when he looked at me and blurted out:

"Hey, I know you. You're the girl from the internet—DatesRGreats."

I didn't dare look at my mother, but I have to tell you the evening was starting to pick up, and it was all I could do to suppress a delighted smile. Gene continued on:

"Yeah I emailed you awhile back, but you blew me off. Don't tell me—your screen name is Blondie something or other, right?"

Sally O'Connor asked me if I was doing internet dating. Sharp woman, that Mrs. O'Connor! No matter how I answered that my mother was never going to be able to face her bridge ladies again, so I decided to just smile and go back to eating my garlic stick.

Gene persisted with his questioning, though.

"How's that internet thing working out for you, Blondie? Me, I quit doing it. Bunch of losers out there, you know? A bunch of stuck up ladies. They all think their you-know-what doesn't stink. But I'd be willing to betcha it does!"

At that comment, he and Mrs. O'Connor broke into hysterics and my mother just sat there stone faced. I was trying to place this guy, but honestly didn't remember him. The thing is I normally received anywhere from three to ten emails a day and most of them I rejected, so it was hard to remember them all. Plus I would soon discover that a lot of the guys were putting pictures of themselves online that were fairly old (and they say women are vain). Maybe my buddy, Gene, had done that also. Anyway Mrs. O'Connor was blabbering on that she couldn't believe a handsome man like Gene would have to resort to internet dating which kind of pissed me off because of the implication that I <u>did</u> need to resort to it. Oh well, disastrous evening number three was winding down and as soon as I finished the somewhat stale chocolate cake I was out of there. One good thing came out of the evening though. My mother never again attempted to fix me up with anyone, and I was persona non grata at any of her functions where any friend of hers might be present.

The rest of the week was pretty uneventful. I had two dates that were dismal, and I was really looking forward to hearing from Brian. He finally called a week and a half later and we agreed to meet for a drink at Papa Pia's, the new trendy bar in Costa Mesa. I decided to have my hair weaved and my makeup done by Joni, my new hairdresser, so I looked pretty stunning if I do say so. He was ten minutes late and didn't even apologize. He also had a handlebar moustache which wasn't in his online picture and which definitely turned me off. However he was still fairly cute, had a great smile and an even greater body so I was prepared to overlook his shortcomings. Also he was an articulate conversationalist and very funny so things were looking pretty promising—until our second green apple martini! Brian told me the reason he was late was his son had run away (again) and he got a call from the police in San Diego that they had found him.

"I guess I'm going to have to go down there to get him tomorrow", said Brian grudgingly.

Not exactly the loving father type!

"It's a pain in the ass", he continued, "because now I have to take off work and waste three hours down there with him."

Me (trying to be sympathetic): "What about his mother? Couldn't she pick him up?"

Brian: "Yeah she could if she wasn't so busy boning half the male population of Orange County."

He went on to tell me that his son had run away from home ten times, been busted for selling weed three times and was put in the detention home a couple of times. I noted that the whole situation must be very difficult for him. Actually I didn't know what to say especially after his comments about having to waste three hours on his obviously troubled child.

"I just don't care anymore. I'm so sick of the whole thing with him, and his whore mother has such a shitty attitude, you know? I can't do it by myself."

He talked on for another forty minutes about this, but I kind of tuned him out after about a minute of sensing the conversation was going to last a bit. I really felt sorry for the kid with parents like Brian and the O.C. whore, he really didn't stand much of a chance. I also started wondering if it was too late to catch Fred, the magician.

I decided to just go home and check emails. Only one was semi-promising and I might have rejected him, but I was feeling a little desperate after my date with Brian so I emailed him back with my work phone number. He called me two days later and sounded pretty cool and asked if I'd like to meet him for lunch that day. I really didn't like luncheon dates but agreed to meet him because he really sounded funny on the phone. His name was Gary and he was a 38 year old detective on the vice squad. If nothing else I might hear some juicy stories about his job. He pretty much looked as bland as his picture but he truly was funny and we had a lot of laughs as we waited for our oyster and mushroom tartlets to arrive. I really liked the fact that he asked if I wanted appetizers—that meant he wasn't cheap like some of the guys who make it clear they are paying for the entree only. I was feeling pretty relaxed with him and decided to get up my courage and ask him the big question:

"Since you work in vice, I was wondering if you ever heard of a comic book called Popeye the Pecker Man?"

He almost choked on his oyster at that one!

"Yeah, sure. He's one of you favorites, I take it?" Gary said this jokingly (I think)

Me: "No, of course not. I never even heard of the book until some perv. IM"d me about this comic book character, and I thought he was putting me on."

No way was I going to tell him my uncle was into that stuff.

Me: "So do you ever read them?"

Gary: "The comic books? Nah. Actually I haven't worked in vice for awhile."

Me: "Oh really? I thought that's what your profile said you did for a living. So what are you doing now?"

Gary: (squirming in his seat) "Actually I've been on unemployment for the last three months."

Me: "Well I guess it's none of my business what happened." (but you damn well better tell me why you lied)

Gary: "No, I don't mind talking about it. My ex left me without any explanation a few months ago, and I just couldn't go to work and so they fired me."

Me: "How awful for you! How long did you not go to work before they fired you?"

Gary: "Well I didn't call in for the first three days, but then I did call and tell them I needed an emergency leave of absence. The department has all these dumb assed rules of protocol you have to follow and I just wasn't in any mood to do what they wanted me to do. A week later I get a letter from them telling me that they assume I have quit since I haven't reported for work in two weeks. I called them back and told them that was bullshit and I'd see them in court. But the truth is I didn't have the energy to fight city hall, as they say, so I just started collecting my unemployment. Guess I need to change my internet profile—just keep forgetting. Anyways, now I'm thinking of a new career."

Me: "What type of career are you thinking of pursuing?"

Gary: "Don't know. Maybe I'll call your friend, Fred, to see if he has any openings in the fire-eating business!"

Suddenly his humor wasn't so humorous. There was a long lull in the conversation, and I remembered why I had a rule about not having meals with guys on first dates. The waiter was taking forever to come back for our order and I had already planned on bailing out of there with just my mediocre oyster and mushroom tart when Gary started the conversation rolling again.

Gary: "It took me awhile to work things out in my head about my ex, but I'm totally over her now. That's why I'm back on the dating scene."

Me: "How long were you married?"

Gary: "We weren't married, but we lived together for almost six weeks. I felt so connected to her, it might as well have been six months, you know?"

Not really, I thought. But I did know this guy was a flake and told him I had to get back to work and really was full from the appetizer. Gary pointed out that I had barely touched it so I felt compelled to lie and tell him that I had an eating disorder and got full very easily. Should I have felt some concern about my increasingly amazing ability to lie to guys without batting an eyelash? Anyway Gary nodded understandingly. His "ex" had an eating disorder also!

I went back to work feeling very dejected but when I checked my emails from work there were two guys who sounded promising, so maybe things were looking up. Marv was a computer programmer who lived in Thousand Oaks, but was willing to drive down here to meet me. That should have set off warning signals right away, but I was a naïve internet gal and agreed to meet him for ice cream at The Ice Palace in Tustin. They had my absolute favorite ice cream and you could add any kind of candy to it to make it even more fattening if you wanted to. Marv phoned me on my cell to tell me he was stuck in traffic and might be a little late. He was right! He showed up fifty minutes later than our agreed upon time, and I had already finished most of my double fudge brownie with Reeses Pieces (what else?) when he arrived.

Marv: "I'm so sorry, Cyn. You don't mind if I call you Cyn, do you? Of course, I'll pay for your ice cream. It looks fantastic, can I have a bite?"

This guy talked faster than the guy in the commercial about phone service and I never could respond to tell him that yes I did mind him calling me Cyn. Since all I had left of my cone was one bite, I let him finish it, especially since he did apologize for being late. When he got up to get his ice cream, I noticed that his but was just a little too big for my liking, but overall he wasn't too bad in the looks department. When he smiled I discovered his teeth could have used some of those whitening agents they had now, but of course didn't mention it to him. He ordered the same thing I did which was annoying because I was hoping he'd get the butterscotch caramel twirl. That was the only flavor I still hadn't tried. Plus I took Marv for being very unadventurous since he chose the "safe" ice cream that he had already tasted. We hadn't even begun our conversation and he already had three strikes against him. I decided to get the messy stuff out of the way up front so there'd be no surprises later.

Me: "How do you like programming?" (my sneaky way of finding out of he, like Gary, had quit working and was on the public dole.)

Marv: "It's pretty challenging. Some days I get involved in a problem and I'm there for ten hours and don't even realize the time has gone by."

Good he was a stable worker. He blabbed on and on for ten hours without ever taking a breath, I swear, about his job, but I had tuned him out a long time ago because I was worried that he might have a Thousand Oaks whore with whom he conceived a troubled child like Brian.

Marv: "Anyway we should be coming out with it soon."

I, of course, had no idea what "it" was because I hadn't been listening so I mumbled something about how great it would be when "it" came out and quickly changed the subject.

Me: "I think I remember reading that you've never been married?"

Marv: "No never. I was engaged but we broke it off and

we're still friends because I believe you should always keep your friendships going even when the passion has left."

Again he started blabbering on about his former fiancée for another twenty minutes and again I wasn't listening. He had to be the fastest talker I had ever seen, and when did this man stop for air? The entire time he was talking I was thinking that he was only 35 so not a big deal that he had never been married and he hadn't mentioned any weirdo kids so I felt pretty safe. When I finally managed to squeeze in a comment, I told him it was good that he discovered that before he got married.

Marv: "Discovered what?"

Oops. I was still back on the passion not being there and he had obviously moved on way back in the conversation. He agreed and said that in the ten years they had been together he had never been able to get her to orgasm without using some mechanical device. That was pretty much it for me and Marv. First of all, any guy who is with someone for ten years before they discover the passion isn't there is a little out of touch with reality. And secondly, and more importantly I might add, his not being able to bring her to orgasm was just way too much information to share on a first date.

Three days later I met Mat for a drink at Goosey Loosey in Irvine. Mat was 42, tall, nice looking and had the most beautiful clothes and car (a 2000 Range Rover). I was grateful that I had put on my red and white sundress with the wrap around shawl because it was a perfect color for me and fit me like a glove. Mat was one of these people that takes over a room the minute he enters. His voice was just a teensy bit too loud, but I could forgive him anything because he was so adorable looking.

Mat: "I had a hellish day! Three of my agents lost multimillion dollar deals and my tailor didn't have the suit I'm wearing to Copenhagen finished like he was supposed to."

Mat owned three real estate companies all in the Irvine/ Newport Beach areas and did ok for himself. He was very sophisticated and I actually had seen his television commercials before so I was pretty impressed to be seen with him. Also drinks at Goosey Loosey started at $15 and the average drink was more like $25. Only the crème de la crème of Orange County society went there—it was sort of a modern day speakeasy for the well to do.

Me: "You're going to Copenhagen? How fun!"

As soon as the words left my mouth I wanted to kick myself for saying something so juvenile. I should have said "it sounds divine" or "how absolutely marvelous" or some other sophisticated thing that wealthy people are always saying instead of "how fun". Mat didn't seem to wince or anything so I was hoping he wasn't too bothered by it. Then I vaguely remembered seeing a profile on him in a local paper sitting next to a twenty something so I figured he probably chased after the young ones and was accustomed to hearing this type of banter. Anyway back to our conversation.

Mat: "Yes I have a business meeting so I decided to combine a little business with medical procedures."

Uh oh! This could be bad news already.

Me: "Medical procedures?"

Mat: "Yes. I'm not one to present facades to anyone I go out with. I believe in putting my cards right out there on the table and dealing with any situation right on.

Me: (hesitantly) "Right, as do I. What sort of cards are you putting out there, Mat?"

He laughed a little. The laugh sounded pretty forced and really nervous to me.

Mat: "Your humor just absolutely intrigues me."

See what I mean about the wealthy and how they express themselves? (not to mention how easily they can change the subject and think you won't notice).

Me: "Good, I like being intriguing. What are these medical procedures you're having to deal with in Copenhagen, if you don't mind my asking?"

Mat: "Of course not. Like I said I'm a "no holds barred" kind of guy.

I waited for my "no holds barred" guy to say something.

Mat: "Hey can I get you another mocha marshmallow martini?"

Me: "Sure can I have a side of explanations with that martini?"

Mat: "Can I just say again how delightful I find you?"

I gave him my best icy cold stare. "Actually just skip the martini and give me some explanation."

Mat: "Well I have herpes and I haven't been happy with the treatments they've been giving me in the States, and I heard there are some very progressive treatments being done in Copenhagen which our pain in the ass FDA won't approve here so I'm going to check it out."

Me: "Herpes, huh? Those are some pretty heavy duty cards you're laying out there, Mat."

Needless to say our date ended much earlier than old Mat had planned. All the way driving home I thought about what a jerk he was, but yet I was glad he told me up front. With my luck I would have fallen for this idiot and then found out the hard way about his disease. When I arrived home, Heroditus had knocked over my tulips that I just bought and helped himself to a few of them before throwing them up all over the dining room table. Great! There was a message from my mother (who had barely spoken to me since the church dinner disaster). I decided what better way to finish a horrible evening than to call mother. She wanted to tell me about the funeral for Chloe (no, I'm not kidding). Apparently over fifty people showed up and even though the ladies from bridge had all brought pot luck, they weren't expecting such a large turnout and ran out of food and had to go to Kentucky Fried Chicken. Mrs. Rimaldi was mortified that there wasn't enough food to feed the masses but did enjoy my mother's apple/blueberry turnovers (as did everyone else, I guess). After finishing my conversation with my mother, I turned on the computer and had five emails. One out of the five looked like someone I might want to pursue so I quickly answered and then collapsed into bed. Michael, the promising email guy, had left his number so I decided to call him since he never answered back to my reply and the weekend was coming up with me in the minus column for dates. He sounded ok on the phone and we made plans to meet for ice cream (another opportunity to have the caramel butterscotch) Friday evening at 7. Michael was probably a 6 ¼ on the 1-10 scale and talked incessantly. He barely asked me anything about myself which I took as an indication that he wasn't interested. He asked me if I wanted to split a vanilla ice cream with him which made things even worse. Was there no man in Orange County who would buy me a caramel butterscotch ice cream?! Somewhere in the conversation he mentioned his wife (as usual I was tuning him out, but my antennae perked up at the "wife" word).

Me: "Whoa, Michael. Can we rewind the conversation a bit to the point where you said your wife, as in present tense?"

Seems Caroline (his very present tense wife) was in Colorado for the weekend and they had an open marriage so this was his weekend to be open, I guess.

Me: "You put in your ad that you are divorced."

Michael: "When I put that ad in I had filed, but we agreed because of the kids we should stay together for appearances sake but see other people."

Me: "Right, I'm sure the kids are much better off seeing you each date other people and have a phony marriage. Incidentally, how long ago was that?"

Michael: "How long ago was what?"

Me: "How long ago did you file for divorce and put your ad up?"

Michael: "Hmm. I think about a year and a half ago."

Me: "So, what, you've been too busy to change your marital status from divorced to open marriage? Oh wait a minute—

they don't actually have that category of open marriage, do they?"

Michael: "Cynthia, you sound a little bit sarcastic."

I didn't bother to respond because I had already stood up and put my coat on to walk away.

Michael wanted to at least walk me to my car. What a guy!!

I stopped at Clancy's on the way home half way hoping to run in to my buddy, Fred. For a minute I thought I saw someone eating fire in the corner of the bar, but it was just the bartender flambéing a drink for someone. I decided I wasn't thirsty after all, but very much horny and decided to just go home. Heroditus seemed happy to see me, and I realized that I hadn't been spending much time with him lately. Guilt was setting in. Since I had no date for Saturday, I'd stay home and hang with Heroditus. Outside I heard a cat moaning in heat. I'm with you, kitty cat, I thought to myself as I once again prepared to go to bed—alone!

On Sunday I got a pleasant surprise from Timmy who had emailed me awhile back but never called. He wanted to meet me for a drink at Clancy's. Hopefully Fred wouldn't be doing any magic tricks there that evening! Timmy was kind of like his name sounds—a little short with a preppie hair cut and a few lingering freckles from childhood.

Timmy: "It's great to finally meet you. Hey I've been meaning to ask you what happened in your marriage."

Great ice breaker, Timmy! Talk about getting right to the point! Since he didn't even ask if I minded talking about it, I decided it was none of his business and told him some bullshit story that my husband was very jealous and was always accusing me of being unfaithful when I never was and I just couldn't stand it anymore and left him. I was constantly worrying that he was still stalking me. Timmy was looking nervously around the bar when I mentioned that! In an effort to get his mind off some crazy jealous guy attacking him, he then asked me why I never had kids. I couldn't believe how personal this guy was getting after just meeting me two seconds ago. He obviously never read the datesrgreats printout that instructed on proper conversation for your date. Basically you were supposed to discuss light hearted topics such as the weather or the latest movie or your favorite musical group. Politics, religion and your past personal life were strictly taboo. I was going to email datesrgreats and ask them to add not discussing problematic children, wives who are whores and various venereal diseases to the list of taboo subjects. Fortunately I didn't do it because my next date with Shane added a new taboo first date subject—substance abuse! Shane was only twenty-five but told me in his first email that he really liked older women. (Not crazy about the "older" classification of me). When we talked on the phone I asked him what it was about older women that attracted him and his response was: "they just know how to groove, honey." He called me honey all the time, even though I never met him, but it was kind of sexy the way he said it. Anyway we met for a drink at Martini Madness and seemed to be having an okay time. When I was nearly done with my second drink, he asked me if I wanted to go back to his place. I informed him I didn't do that on a first date. Shane thought I was joking and asked if I was still living back in the 70's. After all, he pointed out, we had emailed each other twice and talked on the phone three times before even meeting tonight.

"Why don't we just go for a walk along the ocean? It's such

a gorgeous evening." I said this in a hopeful response to get his mind off what would most likely happen back at his house.

"Dude, I have some awesome stuff at home I want to share with you," was his reply.

"What sort of awesome stuff?, I asked nervously.

"Have you ever free based coke?", he asked sexily.

"No!", I answered not so sexily.

"You have to do it, honey. It's so awesome. You'll never be the same again." Shane said this in his best salesman's voice.

"Shane, do you do this on a regular basis?" I was starting to feel very uncomfortable.

He laughed. "Yeah, what's the problem, honey? You need to chill a little."

"I have no interest in doing drugs and I also can't afford it." I felt so uncool saying this.

Shane looked disappointed and mumbled something about going to the john. He was gone quite awhile and he was flying high when he returned to our table. Gee, I wonder what he was doing in there so long! Anyway that was the end of Shane, and I had to admit that the past few weeks had not been very promising. But I must persevere!

I decided to call Nikki to see how things were going with the annulments but got her answering machine instead. Three days later she phoned me back to say she just got back from Vegas with some friends. Apparently Charles broke off the engagement once he learned of her three previous marriages so her friends took her to the MGM to cheer her up. We talked about going out for a drink to one of the happening spots in Newport to find some potential prospects. The great thing about hanging out with Nikki is I'm a teensy bit superficial when it comes to looks (ok very superficial) and she was enormously superficial about wealth, so we never went after the same guys.

Me: "Hey, Nik, remember when we were younger and we wouldn't even consider having sex with a guy until we got married?"

Silence on the other end of the phone!

Undaunted, I continued---"Then when a few years passed, we would consider having sex if we were engaged to the guy?"

Continued silence. Perhaps she was pondering my intense words of wisdom?

"Then a few more years passed and it would be ok if we were really in love?"

Still no response.

"And then it got to be if you really liked the guy, why not?"

Absolutely nothing!

"Then you got to the point where if he was cute and wore pants, go for it!"

Finally a response from the Nikster: "Oh yeah, I know what you mean."

Nikki and I obviously grew up with different moral standards.

MR. SUPERFICIALITY

It's odd how some of the most significant moments in our life being so unassumingly. It was the Tuesday evening after Easter when I logged on as usual to check emails. Most of them were thumbs down, but I decided to answer one because he looked fairly decent in his picture, and he had gone to the trouble of providing me a link to his ad which made things so much easier for me. (It never occurred to me that this guy was a real professional who had this online dating thing down to a science. I just thought he was being helpful.) I decided to reward him with my phone number right off the bat. I was still pretty early in the online dating, so I never gave out my cell nor home phone, only my work number. After awhile I realized most of the guys had caller ID and knew my home phone when I'd return their calls anyway. But as I said this was early on in my dating experience. The following day I received a message from him but decided to call him in the evening when I had more free time. When I did call him back that night I discovered:

A. His name was Byron Samuelson.
B. He was the sales manager for a bicycle parts company
C. He owned his own home in Irvine.
D. He had just got home from a pretty miserable date.

Byron asked what exactly I was looking for in a guy. I told him I had no preconceived notions but felt I would know when I met "the one". Did Byron have any special qualities he wanted in a woman? You betcha! A whole pisspot full of them! After about forty five minutes of listening to all the various racial and ethnic groups he either would or would not go out with, I decided to change gears with him. What was it about his date this evening, I asked, that he didn't care for? (if he didn't mind telling me, I added). Byron's response? She wasn't sexy. Any normal person would have terminated the conversation with him long ago, but I was anything but normal and he said he liked cats. There was also the fact that I had no date for Friday and it was going to be Friday the 13th which was a little spooky to me. He said he'd call me Friday to reconfirm, and I was less than thrilled about seeing him, but also a little intrigued about a guy who was so forthcoming about his feelings. On Wednesday I talked to Jeffrey who had emailed me the week before and we made plans to go out Saturday so the weekend was shaping up rather nicely again. Jeffrey had an awesome body in his picture and was such a sweet and sensitive guy. Plus going out with a jerk like Byron on the night before my date with Jeffrey would make him even more special when we met for brunch Saturday afternoon. I made arrangements to get my hair weaved and a makeover Saturday morning because I really felt that Jeffrey and I were going someplace (romantically speaking). We had several phone conversations in the past week and could not get together this previous weekend because of it being Easter, and he went to San Diego to be with his family. I decided to go shopping Thursday for a really great outfit to wear to brunch Saturday. Once again I was faced with the dilemma of how to dress for my future husband! There would be no such problem for my Friday night date. Byron wanted sexy and I could oblige him with my only sexy top—a black V Neck with an especially provocative V. I also had bought a leopard type bra that I'd wear under it which was barely visible if I sat a certain way. I arrived home empty handed from my shopping spree and barely slept Thursday night worrying about what to wear for Jeffrey. Friday morning came and went, and no call from Byron. Friday afternoon came and went, and no call from Byron. I did, however, get a call from adorable Jeffrey telling me he couldn't wait to meet me the following day. I decided to make an appointment to also get a manicure and pedicure to look especially stunning for Jeffrey. Unfortunately they could only take me Friday evening at 6:30. It was now 6:10 and still no call from Byron so I figured I was being stood up. (not a big surprise about a moron like Byron). I decided to check my answering machine one last time at work before leaving for my beauty treatment, and alas Byron had honored me with a phone call. When I called him back he said he got stuck in rush hour traffic and accidentally left his cell at work. (phoney story). Anyway we agreed to meet for a drink at 8:30. That barely gave me enough time to get the manicure and pedicure done and put on my sexy bra and top, but I actually got to Saucy's Bar and Grill a little early. Byron's picture was a little hazy so I wasn't exactly sure what he looked like. He had made it a point to tell me not to make it obvious that I didn't know him because he didn't like people to know he was on a blind date. Every guy that walked in I would think: Is this the one? Is this the one? Is this the one? Oh please, God, don't let this be the one! All of a sudden from out of nowhere some guy was standing next to me.

"Hey, how are you doing?", he said.

I was so stunned that I hadn't seen him approach and that he looked so different than what I expected that I blurted out very loudly:

"You don't look anything like your internet picture!"

He probably wanted to strangle me after he had made such an issue about not wanting people to know he did internet dating. Well I wasn't off to a good start with this guy which was too bad. He was unbelievably gorgeous—tall, great body in that 'I work out but I don't make it too obvious that I do" kind of way, sandy blonde hair and the most beautiful big blue eyes I've ever seen. Suddenly I was having difficulty remembering who I was supposed to go out with tomorrow. I apologized for making the comment about his picture and he just laughed and poured me some Reisling from the bottle he had ordered for us. He was a very attractive guy and funny and charming in his own weird little way, and I felt like he was way out of my league. I was so happy I wore the sexy top because his eyes were darting down to my breasts all night long. He didn't even try to pretend he was looking at lint on my blouse. Subtlety was not something this guy knew anything about. After about an hour he asked if I was ready to go. Obviously he wasn't interested in me. Only a goddess would be good enough for him, though, so I decided not to feel too bad about it. On the way home I tried to get up some enthusiasm for Jeffrey, but was having great difficulty getting my mind off Byron, the god. I was just turning off the freeway when Mysterious Voice piped up:

"Wow, he was hot!"

Me: "Yeah, but definitely not interested. His eyes were darting all over the room all night as though he expected Madonna to come and rescue him from me."

M.V. "Well too bad because this guy is the first really handsome guy you've met."

Me: "Not true! Ok, you're right. But I could never get someone like him."

M.V. "No, you couldn't."

Me: "Hey, that's not very nice."

The next day came and went with no call from Jeffrey. What a weirdo he was. I found myself increasingly obsessed with Byron, but felt it pretty unlikely I'd ever hear from him again. Two weeks later there was a message at work. It was "him". He said he had been out of town, but was thinking about me and wanted to know if I'd like to get together for a quick bite. When I called him back he said he'd pick me up at 5. I tried convincing him to just meet at the restaurant because I was slightly nervous about someone coming to my home that I did not know, but he was very persistent so I agreed. He showed up forty five minutes late but looked so gorgeous that I decided to forgive him. (not that he really apologized). He put his arm around me as we walked to his silver BMW and told me how beautiful I looked. A warm and fuzzy feeling was building up inside. On the way to the restaurant he casually brought up sex. Uh oh! The only way to get out of this one was to tell him I would not agree to have sex unless he showed me an aids test.

Byron: "Cool, why don't we go together and both get the test."

What a romantic! I told him I hadn't really been having much sex lately (as in not at all) and he said he hadn't either. My naivete has always kept me from being observant about men, but there was no doubt in my mind that this guy was a player, and I was most likely the latest in a long line of playees. We went to a tapas bar and I ate and drank way more than I should have and was feeling pretty aroused by his hand on my back (and my neck, and my thigh and let's not forget the foot massage he gave me over dessert). Bottom line—I invited him back to my place strictly to watch television. I made it very clear to him that this was the purpose of the invitation. He turned on The Real World and we watched about five minutes before he made his move. I kept reminding myself as his fully-clothed body started vibrating on top of mine that I was a nice girl and nice girls do not have sex on the second date with internet player guys. As he reached his hand under my top and unhooked my bra I continued to remind myself that nice girls do not have sex on the second date with internet player guys. While the jeans were carefully being unzipped and pulled from my body I once again reminded myself that nice girls do not have sex on the second date with internet player guys. Apparently nice girls <u>do</u> have sex on the second date with internet player guys—at least this nice girl did. He left shortly after climaxing and I knew two things had happened:

1. I was in love, and;
2. He did not have a condom on.

I spent the next two weeks alternating between depression and severe depression because "my man" had not called me. Seventy-two times during those two weeks I picked up the phone and began to dial his number but always hung up before the phone would ring. I did have a few very forgettable dates during those two weeks, but all I could focus on was "him". Finally one Saturday afternoon at exactly 5:23 in the afternoon, the call I had longed for came.

"Hey, how's it going?". He said this as though we had just been together the day before.

Well I could play along with his game. "Cool," I said, "how's it going with you?"

"Awesome", said the man I wanted to share the rest of my life with and whose children I longed to bear! "I went kayaking for four days and then we backpacked for another two."

Hmmm. That explains six of the fourteen days I didn't hear from him. He didn't say where he went kayaking and backpacking so maybe he had to drive for several days there and back? That was my hope. He asked if I wanted to come to his place on Sunday for a barbecue. Without even thinking I told him I would and we ended our brief phone conversation.

Mysterious Voice: "You sure know how to play hard to get."

Me: "I'm not in the mood for your sarcasm, M.V., so fuck off!"

Mysterious Voice: "What a nasty tone! I'd think you would be thrilled to have heard from him Finally." (total emphasis on the 'finally')

Me: "My ego has been salvaged somewhat, so yeah I'm happy I heard from him again. And yeah I'm happy that I'm going to see him again. And yeah I'm happy that he's probably going to bone me again. So fuck off!"

And with that, mysterious voice did.

I wore a new tank top (braless, of course to make it easy on the poor boy) and tight shorts to his barbecue the next day. He whistled when he saw me and told me how beautiful I looked. Ooooh, getting a warm fuzzy feeling already! He had some salsa music on and grabbed me and started dancing very sexily with me. I was starving and horny and wasn't sure which need was most prevalent for me. Byron made the decision that a little sex before eating helped work up a better appetite (and burn all of those calories) so that's what we did. Dinner was great and I was looking forward to having him for dessert until he stunned me back to reality by saying he had to go out of town on business the next morning and needed to get packed etc. I offered to help him pack in a desperate attempt to spend a little more time with him, but it was obvious he wanted me to go. Hiding my disappointment, I kissed him goodbye and left. On the way home I realized two things:

1. He hadn't said anything about calling me again, and;
2. He once again didn't wear a condom.

I guess I was so madly in love with him that I never thought much about it until after the fact. Since I was in my early 40's and had never conceived, I felt pretty certain that it would be very difficult to impregnate me so I was probably safe, but from a disease point of view it was not smart on my part to allow him to do this. (No, we never went for that aids test together). Next time I saw him (if there was a next time) I would definitely need to talk to him about this. This time three weeks went by before the magical phone call, and just like before I eagerly agreed to see him the following day. My reasoning was that at least he called a day ahead to schedule with me. I was still doing the online dating thing, but coming up with big, fat zeroes all the time. It was going to be very difficult to ever meet anyone who could compare to this Greek God, which was scary considering the fact that a commitment would be very unlikely from him. Our fourth date was at a movie which was pretty uninspiring, and we stopped for a drink at his favorite bar on the way home. Since it was a weeknight, I knew it would be another In and Out for Byron, but I was mesmerized by him and was his slave princess! Two very interesting things occurred at the end of this date:

1. He actually asked me out for that weekend as he was leaving, and;
2. This time he wore a condom.

Of course the week dragged by and all I could think about was seeing him again on Friday. Friday morning he called and

I practically chirped my hello to him. The chirping ceased very quickly when he told me he was going to have to cancel because his mother wasn't feeling well and he promised to go grocery shopping and make her dinner and stay with her that night. Well what could I say to that? Part of me wanted to believe him and part of me thought it was a pretty lame excuse. If he was telling the truth, it put him in a whole new light—devoted and loving son, not some cold, sex-crazed playboy. I rather liked that conception of him and decided to give him the benefit of the doubt. On a happier note, he did ask if he could come to dinner Sunday night at my place. Sunday night supper and sex sounded great to me so I readily agreed, natch. After I hung up the phone I wondered what he was doing Saturday night that he couldn't see me then. Was his mother still going to need his help Saturday? Yeah that was probably it. He wasn't lying and his mother would still need him Saturday too. But he hadn't said she would need him Saturday. In fact, he hadn't said much of anything. That was so typical of Byron. But he was so adorable I could forgive him for breaking the date even if he was lying. Sunday morning came and went and no call from Byron. Every ten minutes I looked at the clock to see what time it was, and every ten minutes I became more and more pissed off. It was now almost 4 p.m. and I hadn't even gone grocery shopping because I wasn't sure if he was even going to show. At 4:20 he called and said he had fallen asleep and didn't realize how late it was. Even though I was fuming, I decided to forgive him and happily went to the store to purchase the goodies for our dinner. He was almost a half hour late, and dinner was almost burned when he got there. There were two other things that were almost burned—me and his face.

Me: "Did you fall asleep in the sun?"

Byron: "Huh?"

Me: "You said you fell asleep and yet you're sunburned."

Byron: "Oh yeah, yesterday I was boating and my sunscreen doesn't work so well, does it?"

I was beyond pissed at this point. He wasn't taking care of his mother yesterday and probably wasn't taking care of her on Friday either. I barely spoke to him at dinner and he wasn't especially chatty either. He didn't offer to clear the table after our meal but went in the living room and turned on television. What word could be used when pissed off no longer works? I think it hasn't been invented yet, but it definitely has been experienced. When I finished cleaning up I made it a point to sit at the opposite end of the couch from him. He playfully kicked me with his foot. I ignored him. Then he grabbed my hand and attempted to pull me close to him. I pulled away. His nibbling on my ears almost won me over, but I was so angry nothing he could do would work on me tonight.

Me: "You know I've had a really long day and I'm really beat."

A normal person would take a hint, but not a horny normal person.

Byron: "Ok let's go in the bedroom and I'll give you a massage."

Me: "I'm not up for it but thanks anyway."

With that Byron got up and mumbled something about it being cool, and headed for the door. I didn't even get up to see him out. After he left I spent most of the evening crying and ranting into my pillow. What an idiot! There was never anything going between us and this mourning of a pretty much non-existent relationship was way out of proportion. Poor Heroditus hadn't seen me in such a state since that fateful New Years Eve night with Sebastian. He jumped up on the bed to comfort me a bit. After a full week of not hearing from Byron, I decided to call him. After all, I reasoned, I had practically thrown him out of the house and he had been sweet and offered to give me a massage and he was probably really tired from getting sunburned because being out in the sun really zaps you energy etc. etc. He wasn't in so I left him what I hoped sounded like a very confident in myself message and prayed I would hear back from him soon. Three days later he graced me with a return phone call once again cheerful and acting like nothing had ever happened between us. We talked for awhile but ended up hanging up with no definite plans. I was bummed. Well hopefully he'd call me in a day or two and ask me out again. My internet dating had come to a standstill partly because I was rejecting just about everyone who emailed me, partly because I was really busy at work and mostly because I was so in to Byron that no one else existed in the universe. Two days after our conversation I got a phone call—from Cary! I was in an irritable mood and was pretty rude to him. Things weren't going well in the cookie baking business for him, but I could have cared less. Apparently the wealthy Newport Beach socialite stiffed him after he put his heart and soul (not to mention most of his money) into the party for her spoiled brat kid and now he was on the verge of bankruptcy. As I said, I had little sympathy for him partly because I had my own problems and they were much more critical than his stupid cookies and partly because I didn't think he was a very good businessman. He asked if I'd like to see him, and I decided that getting out of the house would do me some good.

Mysterious Voice: "Why are you even bothering with him?"

Me: "I'm hurting. Bad! Real bad! Maybe going out with Cary will take my mind off everything.

Mysterious Voice: "No it won't. It's just going to make you feel bad and Cary feel even worse because his cookie business isn't going well and he doesn't need you to add to his problems."

Me: "So what should I do, call him and break the date?"

For once I had to admit Mysterious Voice was right. I didn't like people using me and I was doing that to Cary, whom I had no interest in. For some inexplicable reason, though, I couldn't bring myself to do the right thing. Cary hadn't changed at all and I pretty much felt that he still had feelings for me. I needed that right now--to know that someone, anyone, had feelings for me. To make a long story short, I ended up messing around with him a little bit. We didn't do the Big I but came damn close. Funny thing is it only made me feel worse and made me miss Byron all the more. It also made me realize that Cary deserved success and happiness and definitely someone who treated him better than this shallow, poor excuse for a human being had. (When I'm miserable, I really can look at myself much more objectively) Another week went by and nothing from Byron. Cary called me a couple of times, but I always made some excuse and even he quit calling. I would still go out from time to time with some new online guy, but my heart wasn't in it anymore. The only one making out on this was Heroditus who got to see me more often than he had since I started dating. I spent most of my evenings crying and most of my days dragging myself from one appointment to the next. In the words of Chandler Bing:

"Could I 'be' anymore pathetic?" Occasionally my state of depression would be elevated to anger when I thought about poor Cary and how he had tried so hard and failed. I was tempted to drive by the Newport Beach socialite's home and toilet paper it, but then I remembered I wasn't in 7th grade anymore. After the anger faded, it was back to depressionville for this senorita. I hadn't felt this empty in years. It was as though I was this non-existent entity that no one cared about. So I wrote:

Nothingness

It's impossible to be this empty. It's not bearable to be this alone. Like the prodigal child I was given plenty. But unlike him I have no home. It's regrettable to be this vapid. It's forgettable, the real me. A breakdown's coming on real rapid. Will anyone even see? It's not easy painting phony smiles on. Light and breezy is the way we must be. Must make sure we know the latest jargon. Or escape into a fantasy. It's uncanny seeing all these people. Laughing, loving full of ecstasy. While I'm socially deformed and feeble. Just this nothingness known as me.

Wow! Could a person feel any lower? I think not! The humor that I once used to deal with these situations was obviously failing me now big time. The only thing that kept me going was a persistent fantasy that I'd run into him. Of course, I'd look really hot when I did and he'd tell me how great I looked and how much he missed me and that he really loved me but had never had the courage to tell me. My humor may have failed me, but my ability to live in lala land hadn't. After a month of unbearable unhappiness, I once again called him. This time he was home and sounded happy to hear from me. He asked if I'd like to meet him for a drink on Thursday and I lied and said I had plans but suggested the weekend. He said he'd be out of town for a week but would call me. Yeah right, I thought. But one week and three days later he did. I was in heaven! We met the next evening for a drink and talked and laughed as though nothing had ever happened between us. As he walked me to his car I felt it was now or never so I invited him to my place. He happily agreed not knowing what awaited him there. As soon as we got in the door, I asked him how he felt about me. Bad mistake! He was as polite as he could be and said I was very sweet etc. etc. but he wasn't looking for any kind of anything right now except having fun. If I wanted more, he just wasn't the guy to be with, he continued. I told him that I already knew he didn't want commitment and all I wanted was to have some fun also. At that point I would have said anything to just keep something going with him. The sex was horrible that evening and when he left I wondered if I'd ever see him again. As each day passed, my hopes of hearing from him grew less likely. I don't know at what point I finally gave up on seeing him again, but eventually I knew it was over. Actually it had never begun. One night I was online and looked at his ad for old times' sake. He was online and I knew what he was doing—finding the next playee for his little game. God, what a fool I was! Once again I took to the computer with a fury to let out my rage at this poor excuse for a human being known as Byron.

Mr. Superficiality

Hey, how's it going? How's your life? How's your love? All those girls you've been snowing that you think nothing of—They'll get back at you someday. Revenge is so sweet. Hope I'm there on that Fun Day to see your defeat! You inhabit my being. You devour my soul. Can't believe that I'm seeing me so out of control. See you're still out there surfing, but can't win that big prize. You just leave them all hurting, Mr. Pretty Blue Eyes. Want to go to a movie? Have a steak barbecue? Snuggle in the Jacuzzi? Honey, just me and you? Sweetie, let's get together. Not right now, but real soon. (If I don't meet someone better) I might call you next June. You inhabit my being. You devour my soul. Can't believe that I'm seeing me so out of control.

Hell hath no fury! I can only blame myself for being so stupid but I think the divorce and everything that happened after that seriously impaired my judgment. At least that's the story I'm sticking to. Eventually I started going out again. It was never the same. I never trusted nor believed anyone I met. I was a jaded internet dating junkie.

IF IT'S DECEMBER, IT MUST BE CHRISTMAS

I glumly walked into the mall after my doctor's appointment. Two months prior I had this same doctor confirm what my home pregnancy test had already pretty much told me. I was carrying Byron Samuelson's child. No point in telling him since he had made it clear to me on our first date that he had no interest in having kids. That would be the ultimate insult for him to reject our child as he had rejected me. I had tuned out the world for the last couple of months and had no idea what was happening in Afghanistan or across the street for that matter. My world revolved around me, me and me and it wasn't a particularly happy world. Other than the pregnancy and the cessation of internet dating (or any other kind of dating) nothing much had changed in my life. My mother was dating a nice guy who she was mainly just friends with. Nikki was once again engaged to some bank vice president and was happily planning yet another wedding. Uncle Nathan was still pretty much annoying, pain in the ass Uncle Nathan. Even though I was not a religious person, I had always loved Christmas. The loud speaker in the mall was playing Joy To The World. "Let every heart prepare Him room." My heart had no room for anyone--just my self pity which I had an abundance of. The crowds seemed more than usual and I was having some difficulty maneuvering through them. Suddenly I realized it wasn't a crowd but rather a long line of people. It couldn't be a line for Santa Claus because he was at the opposite end of the mall. "What's going on?" I asked the person at the end of the line. The woman just nodded to a distant sign. At first I couldn't quite read it but then realized it said: "Cary's Cookies". I gasped. The woman in front of me turned around again.

"It's like this all the time. There's another Cary's at the mall in Laguna, but the lines there are even worse. I heard he's opening another place in Fullerton but I refuse to drive that far. The cookies are great, but I have my limitations."

Tears started streaming down my face and I turned away and walked quickly out of the mall. How did all of this happen so fast for him? It didn't matter. For the first time in months I felt that life wasn't so horrible, that maybe there was occasionally a ray of hope to cling to. The Byrons of the world would always be able to charm their way through life. But every once in awhile, a nice guy like Cary could squeeze his way into the playing field and score also. So yes, Virginia, there really was a Santa Claus and an Easter Bunny and a Tooth Fairy and, oh yeah—a God!

PROLOGUE

It's hard to believe that four years have passed since that fateful New Years Eve with Sebastian. My little cast of characters have assembled for a final curtain call—so here goes!

Mrs. Rimoldi now has two goldfish, Chloe Deux and Chloe Trois. Rumor has it that Chloe Trois is a male. So can Chloes Quatre, Cinque and Seis be far behind? Nikki met a count while skiing in the Italian Alps and married him three weeks later. (Her banker fiancée broke off the engagement to marry his babysitter.) Ten months after the happy exchange of vows she was back in the States with the phone number of her favorite divorce attorney in hand. Uncle Nathan went to

Connecticut to visit my sister and her family and decided to stay. Apparently the miserable, blustery winters agreed with his crotchety disposition. Believe it or not, I kind of miss the old curmudgeon. Mother still sees her gentleman friend named Frank, but I continue to think it's strictly platonic. Cary's cookies are now sold nationwide and will soon be in Europe and Asia. I've never seen nor heard from him since he made it big and often wonder if he even remembers me. Sometimes I imagine running into him (when I'm dressed perfect and my hair and nails are done, of course). Fred, the fireater, is now doing a second rate act in a third rate casino hotel in Vegas. Unfortunately I did run into him. Byron apparently fell off the face of the earth. (at least I hope he did). A friend of a friend of a friend told me Sebastian tired of his alternative life style and is now dating his 20 something dental hygienist.

Oh yeah—as for me, I suffered a miscarriage in January after my affair with good old Byron and was briefly hospitalized. One of the orderlies took a liking to me and started calling after I left the hospital. He's overweight, never finished college, dresses far too casual for my liking, has little money and is an aspiring singer. Actually he's quite good, and I really think he should go on American Idol (except I think he's too old). Mother isn't thrilled about me seeing him because he's 14 years younger than me. But we're madly in love so who cares what anyone thinks? Heroditus is happy because I'm not out running the streets with internet guys anymore and he really loves Scotty (my new man). So all in all this little story has a somewhat happy ending. But we can't end without one final musing from Mysterious Voice.

M.V.: "A somewhat happy ending! This is so syrupy I feel like having some ice cream to go with it. It's just like the bullshit we see on television and some movies. I mean I wanted to puke when I watched the final episodes of Friends and Sex and the

City. Rachel walks in to Ross's apartment as he's chanting "Get off the plane, get off the plane", and she quietly says "I got off the plane." Really, Rachel? You magically timed your entry just as Ross is trying to leave you a cell phone message? The airline company is willing to stop the acceleration of the plane to let you go see your on again off again boyfriend/father of your child? And don't even get me started about Mr. Big suddenly flying to Paris to find Carrie and tell her that after six years he's finally decided to commit? In a megacity like Paris, we're supposed to believe that Big bumps into her in her hotel lobby two seconds after she and the Ruskie split up? I'm really glad that life doesn't imitate art, but what about all the poor little teenage girls who watched these two shows and think this is how life works? These little saps may one day find themselves alone after their husbands leave them for someone younger, prettier, more intelligent and sexier. Then they might wait around for six years for the louses to come back and tell them 'We got off the plane!' Every single person you came in contact with has had their made in heaven resolution to their problems. And this Scott dude? You're in love with him?!!! It's all just too overwhelming. Uncle Nathan is happy, your mother is happy, Carey is happy, Heroditus is…."

This time I'm shutting off Mysterious Voice! Because for the first time in several years, life is very, very, very good!

Lenny & Holly

Leonardo (Lenny) Testa wasn't the type of boy a proper mother wanted her daughter to be seen with. Granted, from a purely physical perspective, he was one hot item with his muscular arms, firm buttocks, jet black hair and blue-grey eyes. And let's not forget the ever-present bulge that he loved showing off by wearing slightly snug jeans. The problem was he wasn't from the right sort of family. He lived in a modest three bedroom, two bath 50's style home with his parents and two sisters. His father was a construction worker and his mother worked part time in the nearby Italian deli. When the weather turned cool, his father would head south to find more work, sending money home whenever he could. On his mother's day off from the deli, she would make homemade spaghetti with meatballs that she ground with her old fashioned meat grinder. Dessert was often tiramisu or fried dough balls with cinnamon, sugar and fennel seed sprinkled on the balls as soon as they came out of the hot oil. During the Easter holiday she would make baby doll egg bread and a pastry filled with hot sausage and potatoes. They never lacked for food on the table and always had clothes in their closets that usually came from the type of stores that lower middle class people frequented looking for that always desired bargain. Lenny wasn't a bad boy, just restless as were so many eighteen year olds trying to find answers to questions that they weren't even sure they understood. On his seventeenth birthday, he bought a motorcycle with the money he saved working on the weekends at the deli with his mother. More often than not, the townsfolk would see a lady on the back of the bike with Lenny cruising down the main street of town. School didn't interest him much, and after graduation he still worked part time at the deli and helped out at a local auto shop when they needed him. College wasn't an option that he even desired, which was the norm for the Oilers from his high school. The Oilers were the blue collar kids who were into fast cars and even faster girls and never thought much about the future.

Holly Nicholas celebrated her 16th birthday with a steak dinner at Romanoff's with her three best girlfriends, her parents and her brother and older sister, Katrinka. It was a bittersweet celebration since Katrinka would be leaving for her first year at Lutheran College in Minnesota in just two months. It would be the first time anyone in the family had been away from home (except for the frequent business trips her father made as regional sales manager for a computer company) and Holly already missed her big sister before she even left. Every summer Holly and her friends volunteered for day camp at her church and never missed Sunday services at 1st Lutheran Church. She was part of The Debs, the upper middle to upper class group of girls who were always prom queen or homecoming queen or on the student council etc. etc. They never socialized with the Oilers. Holly's Lutheran upbringing taught her to be kind to everyone so she would smile at The Oiler boys when she saw them in the hall, but never anything more than that.

Cassie Nicholas, Holly's mother, had just returned home from a Parent Teacher meeting when she received a most alarming phone call from her friend, Anna Dougherty. One of Anna's friends had seen Holly riding on the back of Lenny Testa's motorcycle earlier in the day. This was alarming on two counts—Cassie broke her leg many years ago in a motorcycle accident and still had a lingering fear of the vehicles; and she certainly did not want her daughter associating with the Testa boy. She really knew little about the Testas, only that she didn't want her daughter associating with them, and pondered how to broach the subject with her younger daughter when she returned home from an errand for her brother.

Holly, like many other girls at West High School, had noticed Lenny Testa when she was still a freshman. He always seemed to be surrounded by his Oiler friends or some hanger on groupie girl. She would smile at him and he would usually return the smile. In the summer before her sophomore year in school, she and her girlfriends went to a nearby lake to swim and she saw Lenny there with a girl. The two were having a picnic on a blanket and Lenny was bare from the waist up. Holly felt a warm sensation in her body which she had never experienced before as she watched him and the girl laughing and drinking beer. When Lenny began kissing the girl and removing her bikini top, the warm feeling in her body intensified and she quickly ran to find her girlfriends. Sometimes she would wake up at night and see Lenny taking the girl's top off and wishing it was her. On those nights, it was quite difficult for Holly to go back to sleep. She began praying that the thoughts she was having and the tingly warm feelings in her body would go away. For some reason, they only got worse. One year later she was at the same lake and again saw Lenny on the same blanket but with a different girl. The feelings in her body would not be silenced any longer, and she bravely walked over to the couple and said hello. When Lenny looked at her with his steely eyes, she spilled her coke all over the blanket and partially on Lenny. She tried to wipe some of the ice off his leg and immediately noticed his bulge getting really big. It was more than she could bare and she stammered an apology and ran off. That night some of the Debs were having a barbecue at the lake, but Holly lied and said her period had come and she couldn't go. It wasn't that she thought Lenny might still be there, but the memory of his body was too much for her to bear. A few days later she was at the soda shop having a chocolate soda with double whip cream when Lenny walked in. He invited her to go for a ride on his motorcycle and she eagerly agreed. Holly had never been interested in bad boy types and certainly an Oiler boy wouldn't appeal to her. But the sexual desire she felt completely overpowered her and when he invited her to go to the lake after their motorcycle ride she instantly said yes. As they rode to the lake she felt wet inside thinking of the infamous blanket and of Lenny removing her top and kissing her. They talked briefly and Lenny offered her a beer. Holly didn't care for the taste of beer so just had one or two sips. That was all she needed and Lenny made his move. There was no resistance on her part—just pure excitement and unbelievable pleasure. She had promised herself she would only allow him to get to first base, but that afternoon Holly Nicholas and Lenny Testa hit an out of the park homerun!!

Even though Holly felt terrible guilt and shame at what she had done, she would sneak off for a ride with Lenny on a fairly regular basis. Their "rides" always ended the same way. Holly wasn't worried because Lenny always wore a condom. She did start to worry when she was over a month late with her period. There was absolutely no one in the world Holly could entrust this to, and the stress and fear she was feeling was boiling over in her young body. Katrinka called home one day to talk to the family and caught Holly alone at home and crying hysterically. When Katrinka heard the news, she told Holly she knew of someone who could take care of the "problem" without anyone knowing. Holly considered how easy it would be to just make this go away without anyone being the wiser. In the end she couldn't do it and decided to tell Lenny first before anyone else. Since he was Italian, Holly fully expected him to go into a rage and throw things and swear and maybe even hit her like they used to do in the movies. Lenny didn't say a word. His eyes glassed over and he just stared into space. Holly wasn't sure if this was a good or bad sign. She was hoping her family would have the same calm (or numb) reaction. It could have been worse, but it wasn't too good. Her mother started crying and her father just stormed out of the room. Her brother said he was going to kill the son of a bitch which prompted her father to come back into the room to chastise her brother for using such language. The fact that he wanted to kill the father of Holly's baby didn't seem to disturb her dad too much. Anyway to make a long story short, Holly's family contacted Lenny's family and it was decided between the two families that the couple should wed. Holly and Lenny didn't have any voice in the matter, and two weeks later they were married in a most private ceremony at city hall. Holly didn't even get to buy a pretty suit for the day, much less a beautiful bridal gown. At least her parents took everyone out to dinner afterwards, but it was a pretty strange dinner to say the least. Married life began for these two practical strangers in the extra bedroom that Katrinka vacated when she went off to college. Lenny was miserable living there and as soon as he had enough money saved from the two jobs he now worked, the newlyweds moved into a one bedroom apartment above a garage in a so-so part of town. Holly always read about how young couples began their marriage in difficult circumstances barely making ends meet but then how they always looked back on these times as the happiest years of their marriage. If these were the happiest years, Holly couldn't bear to think what would follow! When she didn't have morning sickness (which lasted all day-who was the genius that called it morning sickness?) she tried learning how to cook, grocery shop, keep their tiny apartment clean and study for her GED. She dropped out of school before she started showing because it was just too humiliating to face her friends. Everyone knew by this time, but she had a new and very different life from her old chums and rarely talked to them. Lenny was usually too exhausted by the time he got home to engage in that same behavior that got her into this mess to begin with. Her hormones were totally out of control and she probably would have humped a lamp if she could have. It was understandable that Lenny wouldn't find the fatso she now saw everyday in the mirror as desirable, so she just drudged through each day trying to focus on her many tasks. By the eighth month of her pregnancy she was miserable all the time, but still kept a neat home, made sure there was a healthy (if somewhat scarce) meal on the table and finished her high school studies ahead of schedule. When the due date drew near, she packed her bag for the hospital and made sure there was extra food in the refrigerator for Lenny during her absence. Erin Testa arrived into the world two days late. Labor was really difficult for Holly, but once it was over she was fine and eager to hold her new little bundle. Lenny and everyone in the family were actually excited about the baby, and Holly thought maybe all of the horrible past was behind her now. Since Lenny still worked two jobs, it was up to her mother and mother-in-law to help out. They both tried to outdo each other in the execution of their grandmotherly duties. Holly was thrilled that they loved her little Erin as much as she did. After Holly received her GED, she enrolled part time in a community college. It would take her forever to get a bachelors degree, but at least she was trying. She found it annoying that Lenny had no ambition to do anything with his life. She found it annoying that he did very little to help around the house on his day off. Most of all, she found it annoying that the only time he really paid attention to her was during their lovemaking which now occurred quite regularly. One day she called Katrinka and poured her heart out to her about all these things. Katrinka lived in a completely different world of studying, partying and dating. Of course, she could not relate at all to Holly's problems. After three years of going through the motions of marriage, Holly had enough and told Lenny she wanted out. His reaction was pretty much the same as when she told him she was pregnant. She thought he would at least cry because he wouldn't have Erin in his life everyday, but he didn't.

Lenny was actually a loving father to Erin—something Holly hadn't noticed when they were together. He dutifully picked her up every other Friday right on time and dropped her off again late Sunday evening. The Testas helped Lenny with the baby since he was still working two jobs to help support Erin, even though he now lived back at home with his parents. Holly occasionally saw her old schoolmates, but between going to college and caring for a young one, she didn't have a great deal of free time. One day Cassie greeted her daughter at the door with a huge smile, something she never did. It seems Katrinka had a long weekend so she thought it would be an excellent idea for the three of them to meet in New York and have a girls only weekend. Cassie had already arranged for Lenny to take Erin a day early, and Holly was ecstatic. She hadn't had any real vacation for so long, it would be pure heaven. Holly's dad was again on a business trip, so everything worked out perfectly. There was so much catching up to do and, of course, the requisite oohing and awhing over the latest pictures of Erin. Cassie took her two daughters to an elegant bar on the Upper East Side and Holly had a Green Apple Martini—it was the most exotic drink she had ever tasted. A few minutes later the waiter arrived with a bottle of Dom Perignon compliments of the man at the table next to them. The girls teased their mother that she still had it going on, since the gentleman was obviously older (in his forties at least!) and it was assumed he was interested in Cassie. It was unanimously agreed that they should invite him to their table to help drink this most exquisite champagne. His name was Keith Blackman and he was an aeronautics engineer living in Connecticut. He frequently came to New York on business, but infrequently met three such beautiful women on his trips. They three ladies blushed in unison at his corny line, but all secretly hoped he was sincere. It was increasingly obvious that he had not sent the expensive bottle of bubbly to gain the attention of the mother, but rather her lovely youngest daughter. The man was most mannerly and asked permission to call Holly which she shockingly agreed to. Over the next several months, Keith always found some excuse to come to Kentucky on "business" so he could see her. He wined and dined her and bought her expensive gifts. Cassie was not pleased with the big age difference, but saw that her daughter was falling in love with him and decided he was a definite improvement over Lenny. Unlike the first wedding in civil hall, this one was a large and lavish affair held at the Westchester Country Club. Holly felt a little silly wearing a designer gown with a train and veil but reveled in her big day. Erin was the flower girl and looked adorable beyond belief. She started crying two minutes before the ceremony so Holly carried her down the aisle as her father escorted the two of them. Following a honeymoon in Tahiti, Holly and Keith settled into his large estate in Connecticut. She was so busy with Erin, Keith and all the activities she now participated in at the country club that she had little time to feel homesick. Lenny was now only able to see his daughter during the summer. Holly never saw nor talked to him since her parents always drove Erin back to Kentucky to be with her dad and drove her back again in September. By now, Holly's father was retired and he and Cassie loved to travel. Katrinka had a business degree and was living and working in New York City. Sadly, Holly didn't get to see her as often as she would like, but they always got together for Christmas and Easter. As the years went by, Erin developed into a beautiful and accomplished young lady. She had excellent grades, played a mean game of tennis and was head cheerleader at Westchester High School. Holly had high hopes that she would go to Yale or Princeton and was quite shocked when her daughter informed her that she wanted to go to a rather obscure college in Savannah Georgia. Lenny had moved there several years earlier and had opened an Italian restaurant. Eventually the entire Testa family joined him there and all worked in the restaurant. Holly knew Erin loved spending her summers there, but was stunned that she actually wanted to go to school there. Perhaps she had met someone and fallen in love? Erin assured her mother that was not the case. Holly felt hurt that Erin preferred living near her father, but assumed it was just a passing phase and agreed to let her apply to the university. Keith had been working very long hours for the past year, and Holly suddenly felt lonely for the first time in many years. She decided to do some spring cleaning (even though Jessie, the cleaning lady would be at the house the following day). It was rare that she went into Keith's home office, but she decided to start in that room. He had forgotten to log out of the computer, and she noticed several emails from "lipstouching". Her heart started pounding, but she told herself she was being silly. It was probably one of Keith's golf cronies who was using a sexual email address. The wise thing to do would be to leave the room and pretend she hadn't seen anything. Perhaps she could ask Keith that night which one of the guys from the club used that funny name. Curiosity got the best of her and she opened one of the emails. It wasn't a golf buddy. It was a love email from a woman. She read one or two more and felt sick to her stomach. Her body was ice cold and she was shaking all over. At that very moment, the doorbell rang. Cassie was at the door and Holly was in no state to see her. Her mother saw her at the window, so she had no choice but to come to the door. She had forgotten that her mother was coming over for lunch before she left to go to New York to see Katrinka. Never losing the motherly instinct, Cassie demanded to know why Holly was in such a state. When Holly told her that Keith was having an affair, her mother did not seem terribly shocked and simply told her that she should look the other way. After all, she had a wonderful home and a comfortable life and her husband was probably just having a little fling as so many men do. Women weren't the only ones to get menopausal, she informed her daughter. She and Holly went to the club for a drink and Holly decided to take her mother's advice for now until she could figure out what to do. Her first major decision was to go to Savannah with Erin to see the university and give a final approval of her daughter's plans. She wondered if she would see Lenny and how he might look after all these years.

Savannah was an absolutely charming city, and the people were so friendly and down to earth. Holly immediately understood why her daughter wanted to spend her college days here. They were staying at a lovely old hotel and Holly was going to have dinner at a nearby restaurant owned by a celebrity chef that evening since Erin was spending the evening with her father's family. Erin had begged her mother to join them, but Holly felt it wasn't appropriate even though she was a little curious about Lenny. She knew he had never remarried and his restaurant was fairly successful, but not much else. Erin asked her mother to at least come and see Lenny's restaurant before they left the next day, and Holly acquiesced to her daughter's wishes. Testa's Trattoria was a medium sized restaurant and very simply decorated. Since it was in between the lunch and dinner crowd when they arrived, Holly assumed she might not see any of the Testa family. Erin's grandmother spotted the two of them and came over and warmly hugged them both. She had aged quite a bit since last seen by Holly, but she still worked six days a week for her son making meatballs and sausage for the adoring clientele. After being invited to sit for a quick drink before Holly had to leave, Mrs. Testa talked on and on asking Holly a million questions about her life in Connecticut with her supposedly adoring husband. These questions brought Holly back to the unpleasant recent events in her life that she hoped to avoid temporarily with her little sojourn to Georgia. Tears were welling up inside her that she was making every human effort to suppress. Then across the room she saw him—he was talking to one of the waiters and hadn't noticed them. Mrs. Testa called to her son and as he walked towards them he suddenly saw Holly for the first time. They exchanged pleasantries and Erin asked her father to show Holly the restaurant. She and Mrs. Testa concocted some lame excuse for not accompanying the two former spouses, so off they went. Holly couldn't imagine that Erin was trying to get them back together again since Erin had no idea of the problems in her marriage. Anyway after a brief tour and a feeble attempt at catching up on their lives over the past fifteen years, they arrived back at the table to find Erin and Mrs. Testa gone. Lenny offered to provide her with dinner, but Holly declined stating she already had dinner plans. Since he obviously couldn't leave her sitting alone, he joined her in the tiny booth and had his bartender open two beers for them. Holly playfully reminded him what happened the last time they had two beers and they both laughed. She ended up having dinner at the restaurant with her still very handsome ex husband and seeing most of his family during the course of the evening. When had she laughed so much and felt so happy? She couldn't remember. Back to reality the following day as she returned to all the sadness and hurt she had left behind. After a week or two of Keith coming late "from work", she confronted him. He, of course, lied and they had the first real argument of their long married life. Women in her mother's generation probably did learn to look the other way and bear the anger and pain in exchange for the comforts and security that went with marriage. Holly couldn't bear the thought of a second failed marriage, but she also couldn't live a lie. Once again she was in the divorce court, this time with a pricey lawyer since Keith was fighting her bitterly over all their "things" accumulated over fourteen years of marriage. Holly had taken a job as a senior account executive (a position her father recommended her for to some former clients of his) and loved the work but hated going home to the big empty home (part of the divorce agreement). When Erin telephoned her from Savannah to invite her down for Christmas, she jumped at the opportunity. She told herself it was strictly to be with her daughter, but in her heart she knew her child's father was also very much on her mind. It was the first Christmas Holly spent away from her family, but she was spending it with her other family. They even went to church together on Christmas Eve. Holly had never been in a Catholic Church before and was noting the similarities to her own faith. During her two week stay, she found herself falling back in love with Lenny and wondered if he felt the same. There was a certain amount of guilt about all of this, since the ink on her divorce papers had barely dried. When she returned home, she did the cowardly thing and sent Lenny an email telling him in a somewhat guarded way how she felt about him. Two days went by and there was no reply. She cried into her pillow at her foolishness for sending him the love note. Then on the third day she saw a reply from him. "How about moving here and let's see what happens." That was all he could muster up? Did he really think she would sell her beautiful home, leave her friends and comfortable lifestyle to move to a strange city to see what maybe, possibly, perhaps could happen?

Turns out, yes she would!

New Years at the Michaelson's

A teardrop fell on the pages of the slightly worn notebook paper. Maura Michaelson had pulled out the notebook just as she had every year for the past thirty years to add a new page to the recipes that she and Mark had developed. Would Mark still be around for them to add a new recipe this year? That question had been haunting Maura ever since she first learned that the growth Mark had discovered was cancer. Doctors said that the good news was they had caught it early and removed it and there was no sign that it had metastasized. They recommended Mark begin chemotherapy as soon as possible. Mark had other ideas. His best friend, Martin, had passed away three years ago and the memories of his suffering from the chemo were still fresh in Mark's mind. So Mark decided to try an experimental program of herbs, exercise and healthy eating that he had read about online. Borrowing from the feminists' mantra, he told the family that it was his body and he was going to do what he thought was best for him. Neither Maura nor their two sons, Michael and Mathew, were consulted in his decision. Maura pretended to support his self-imposed therapy, but she often felt that after thirty years of marriage his body belonged a little bit to her also.

Every New Years day for the past thirty years, she and

Mark had created a recipe containing at least one ingredient from each of them that had a special meaning to them, and they would make that dish to begin their new year together. She hadn't even asked Mark what, if anything, they should make this year. As she scanned through the pages hoping for some creative inspiration, Mark walked in.

"Oh, it's almost that time again, babe. Are you trying to get a head start on me with your ingredient?" Mark was very cheerful as he usually was and she would respond in like manner, somewhat relieved that the subject had been broached finally.

"No cheating!" he jokingly called out as he left the room as abruptly as he had arrived.

ARTICHOKE DIP

Her mind was completely blank and she closed the notebook, but opened it to the first page for some reason, though she wasn't sure why. A smile brightened up her face as she read the very first recipe they ever entered in the book for their first New Years together as husband and wife. She had neatly printed it and put it in laminated paper to preserve it. Rather than the usual sauerkraut or black eyed peas, she and Mark decided they wanted to create their own tradition to bring them good luck in the new year. They decided to have a contest to see who could pick out an ingredient that had a special meaning first, and then they would create a recipe from that ingredient. Maura had spent one of the happiest years of her life as a child living in Castroville, California. Since her father was in the military, the family moved around quite often and Castroville was probably the longest she stayed in any one place. It was, and still is, the artichoke capitol of the world. Maura's mom found more ways to prepare artichokes than probably anyone else's mom anywhere. The light bulb went on in Maura's mind as she reminisced about her childhood days of eating artichokes pretty much nonstop.

"I've got mine," she proudly announced to her husband of five months.

"Oh no, I've been one-upped by a "woman"!, he jokingly responded.

"Well, cooking is the woman's domain, so I'm not too"-he never had a chance to finish his sentence because she threw a wet washcloth at him and started chasing him with her broom as he ran from the room laughing and screaming for someone to help protect him from the crazy lady.

Mark actually had already picked out his ingredient also, but let Maura have the honor of winning. When Maura saw the piece of crumbled paper that was in the waste basket with 'sour cream' written on it, she knew Mark had really been first. She asked him why he chose sour cream.

"Oh my mother was part Russian and for the first real meal I could swallow after my tonsillectomy she made me Beef Stroganoff. I remembered how great that tasted after the endless jello and chicken broth I had to endure so I thought I'd honor my mommy with using sour cream in our recipe."

Maura gave him a big kiss and it was right then and there that they decided both ingredients should be used. So they made a dip using both the artichokes and sour cream and bought a package of tortilla chips and some inexpensive sparkling wine and toasted their first New Years Day (with the certain knowledge that there would be so many more to follow). Money was scarce in the early years and the following New Years Day recipe wasn't much more elaborate than the first one had been.

LEMONADE PUNCH

The Michaelson family had a huge lemon tree in their back yard when Mark was growing up that he was always forced to help prune. Despite his constant complaining that he would rather be out playing ball with his pals, he loved the taste of the fresh squeezed lemon juice. Maura and Mark decided that lemons should be included in their second New Years recipe together. Maura didn't need any time to come up with her choice of ingredient:

"When I was ten years old," she explained to Mark, "Daddy allowed me to have my first 'cocktail' at Christmas. I'm sure it was really watered down quite a bit, but I was so proud of being included with the grownups in our Christmas toasting festivities. For an extra special effect, Daddy topped my drink with a maraschino cherry that floated around the liquid and looked so pretty and tasted even better."

Well you can't get much more simple than that—lemonade punch with maraschino cherries! Maura decided to get the punch ready before Mark came home from visiting his parents. Mark came storming through the door, excited as all get out—

"Babe, I got us some fuzzy pussy!" he yelled ecstatically for all of the neighborhood to hear.

"Excuse me?!", Maura feigned shock at his language.

"Fuzzy Pussy, you know Pouilly Fuisse. It's a fancy French wine that will go great in the punch." Mark could barely contain his animated state.

"How did you manage to do that?" Maura knew they couldn't afford any real splurging and was curious. "Ran into an old friend who gave it to me as a New Years present—far out, huh?"

So the "fuzzy pussy" was added to the lemonade punch (along with the artichoke dip and chips), and year two commenced. It was the last New Years Day for just the two of them because two months later Maura discovered she was pregnant. She broke the news to Mark by telling him she could not have any fuzzy pussy in her lemonade next New Years. He let out a loud whoop, picked her up and carried her straight to the bedroom.

PEANUT BUTTER AND JELLY PIE

"Hey, we haven't even begun to think about our recipe and New Years Day is in just a few weeks." Maura was so exhausted with baby Michael that she barely had time to think about combing her hair anymore, much less coming up with a new years' recipe.

"Oh, Babe, after smelling your vomit for six months and now Michael's poopy diapers, peanut butter and jelly would sound good to me!" Mark joked.

"So that's it," shrieked Maura, "we'll make a peanut butter and jelly pie."

"Where did that come from?" Mark figured Maura might still be having the weird cravings she had during her pregnancy.

"Because I've been craving pies for the past two weeks, and you have ignored all the little hints I've been throwing to get me pie, so we're going to make a peanut butter and jelly pie for this year's New Years." Maura had it all figured out.

"One tiny problem, babe--my parents want to come over to see the baby on New Years day, and Mom's allergic to peanuts." "Even better", Maura said mischievously. She neither liked nor disliked Mark's parents and the thought of feeding them something so weird gave her an evil sort of pleasure.

The original plan was to make the crust from scratch, but between taking care of baby Michael, Christmas shopping and trying to keep the house in some semblance of cleanliness, Maura settled for a store bought pie shell. At the last minute, Mark's dad came down with the flu so they didn't want to expose the baby and bowed out of the New Year's celebration. Maura was secretly thrilled that it was just the three Michaelsons beginning yet another new year. It was a perfect day until Maura caught Mark trying to sneak a teensy bit of peanut butter and jelly pie filling on his finger to Michael.

"Are you trying to kill our child already?", she yelled as she licked Mark's finger before he could finish the dastardly deed. "Babe, I just wanted Michael to share in our feast. Calm down, I wouldn't really have tried to give him any. Just wanted to shake you up a bit, lovey."

SCHNITZEL

During those times when it was impossible to stop Michael's crying, Maura would rock him and sing "My Favorite Things" from the Sound Of Music. It always made him go to sleep (sometimes Maura nodded off also in the middle of the song). On one such day, she got the inspiration that Schnitzel should be the next New Years item added to their now increasing menu.

"Mark, we have our entrée now!," she yelled to her husband who was watching football in the other room. "Great, babe.", was his reply. Mark, of course, didn't even hear what she said because the Cowboys were about to try the game winning field goal with only three seconds remaining in the game.

"Honey", she continued, "when the game is over can you run to the store and get me some peppers?"

"Sure, babe." Mark heard store and something beginning with the letter "P" but was too engrossed in the game to ask what it was she wanted. "How many?", he asked as the Cowboys went down to defeat.

"Three or four should do it."

Mark dutifully went to the store and returned home with what he was fairly sure she had asked for—four bottles of paprika.

"What the hell is this?!" Maura couldn't believe what he had brought home.

"Uh, I'm guessing not what you asked me to bring home?" Mark was trying to keep from laughing. "I don't know why I even try to talk to you when you have some stupid ass game on." Maura was also trying not to laugh at his stupid mistake. "Well I imagine you also didn't hear me tell you that my choice for our New Years dish is schnitzel." She was still acting the indignant wife. "Oh, great idea! Now we have a full course meal—appetizer, drink, dessert, and thanks to your brilliant choice the entrée!" Mark was attempting to get back in her good graces, but judging by the exasperated look on her face, he knew he was just stepping deeper and deeper into poo poo. "You already mentioned this, didn't you?" Mark said sheepishly. Maura just glared and walked out of the room. Mark followed her holding two of the bottles of paprika. "I guess I have my contribution to New Years. What do you think, babe?" Maura replied: "Yeah, with all of this paprika I guess we'll be having Hungarian Schnitzel".

HUNGARIAN NOODLES

Mark decided that the following New Years they would have Hungarian Noodles to try to use up at least a little of the paprika he mistakenly purchased. Little did he know that by the time New Years came, they were both nauseous at the sight of paprika. Maura used the paprika every possible chance she had and even put it in a Mexican Mole that she heard about from a friend. Little Michael was eating people food by now, so she had to be careful not to put too much in anything he was having also. They had managed to use one box of the paprika and were trying to figure out how to get rid of the other three boxes.

"It would make a great Christmas gift, babe. Why don't you make up some pretty baskets with goodies in them and we'll give them to our nearest and dearest." Mark was always so helpful when it came to fixing his boo boos. "That's a great idea, Mark! I'm going to get right on that after feeding Michael, bathing him, cleaning up his mess, changing his diaper, feeding him again, cleaning up his mess again—oh, I'm sorry, did that sound sarcastic?!" Maura tried to get her point across with a little humor as often as possible, but she truly was exhausted and looking forward to the day when Michael went away to college.

She did give one of the boxes of paprika to her neighbor who wanted to borrow some one day. Down to just two! That New Years day Mark had promised a big surprise and the entire family was coming by to share New Years dinner with them. Maura was so excited because her parents were in town and going to spend a week with them before taking a cruise to the Bahamas. By this time she had learned to like, if not occasionally love, Marks' parents and was actually looking forward to cooking for the whole gang.   No   one was permitted to bring any side dishes because dinner always had to be about their own tradition. After dinner Mark had everyone come into their tiny living room apartment to announce his big surprise. He had been saving to start his own air conditioning company and now had enough money to go ahead with it. He was turning in his notice the next day at work and had already rented a small commercial space in Berea to set up shop. Everyone jumped up and started hugging and congratulating him. Maura was beyond stunned. While she was aware of his dream and knew he had been putting money aside, she felt he should have at least consulted her first. As she got out of her chair to go over and hug him, (she wasn't one to make a scene in front of others—but wait until they were alone!) she started feeling queasy. Instead of hugging Mark, she ran past him straight to the bathroom and promptly threw up her entire New Years meal! Her guests made an early departure so their hostess could rest, and then she had it out with Mark. She informed him that she was so upset, it caused her to loose her lunch (dinner in this case). Mark, as usual, apologized and tried to console her and promised he would never again even dream of making an important decision without her prior knowledge. He had just assumed she wouldn't care since she already knew of his eventual plan. Maura felt a little guilty and they went to bed that evening holding each other closely. The following day, Maura started feeling queasy and again had to make a beeline for the toilet.

She attributed it to nerves about Mark quitting his job today. When the vomiting continued every day, she decided to go to the doctor. No point in alarming Mark until she knew what was wrong, so she didn't tell him of the daytime vomiting nor the doctor's appointment. When Mark arrived home one evening, Maura greeted him at the door:

"I guess there won't be any fuzzy pussy for me next New Years either!", she announced to her startled husband. "Weren't you using a diaphragm?", Mark asked.

"Guess they aren't foolproof. Not very good timing with you starting your business, huh?", Maura tried to make a joke about it. Mark was his usual affable self and just told her they'd make it work somehow. "And if things really get bad, we can always eat paprika!" At that remark by Mark, Maura promptly ran to the bathroom and threw up!

BRUSSELLS SPROUTS CASSEROLE

Maura's pregnancy was very difficult and the last month was spent in bed most of the time. Her mother flew in from Miami to help with Michael. The heat and humidity were unbearable and for some odd reason, the only food Maura liked to eat was brussels sprouts. The cabbage vegetable gave her gas so bad that no one wanted to be in the same room with her, but she didn't care. On the last day of August, Matthew made his debut at almost 11 pounds. Maura had to have a Caesarean Section to deliver him and pleaded with her mother to stay a little longer until she recuperated from the surgery. Mark was at this point working twelve to thirteen hours every day, and the thought of taking care of two little ones when she was so tired and sore wasn't especially appealing to Maura. By the time her mother left, Maura was pretty much back to normal—normal being getting up at 5 am to make breakfast for Mark and feeding baby Matthew, dressing and feeding Michael, changing Matthew's diaper, trying to coax Michael to use his new potty chair, changing Michael's clothes after he had his tenth accident of the day, doing laundry, feeding the boys lunch and dinner, cleaning up the various spills and breakages that occurred during the day and collapsing into bed at 8 pm. Often she was sleeping when Mark got home. It was a weird relationship, but she loved her family more than anything and tried not to feel too sorry for herself. Mark had decided to have a vasectomy and Maura reluctantly agreed. She really wanted more children, but was exhausted from the two she had, so Mark didn't need to persuade her too much to go along with his decision.

Both of them were much too tired to think of something creative for the upcoming New Year, so they agreed to make a Brussels Sprouts casserole in honor of Maura's pregnancy craving. With a little help from Fannie Farmer and Julia Child, Maura was turning into a fairly good cook (when she had time) and found a recipe for a vegetarian casserole that sounded pretty good to her. This year, it would only be the four of them, which suited Maura fine.

POMMES FRITES

Maura was fanning through a cookbook one day when she saw a recipe for baked French fries with paprika. That might be a good idea for next New Years, she thought. It would not be time consuming and seemed pretty simple to make—two factors that won Maura over, considering that she was still running around after the boys nonstop and had no time for much of anything else. Mark was still working long hours, but business was growing enough that he hired two assistants. He was even talking of renting a larger commercial space. Maura wasn't having any of that!

"Why can't <u>we</u> rent a larger space?", she complained to her husband. "Nah, I don't like that idea.", he responded. Maura frowned and started walking out of the room.

"Hey, what's with the puss, Puss?", Mark had a mischievous smile on his face and Maura knew something was up.

"One of my customers has a wife who works in real estate, and I was telling him to tell her to find a nice big house for me and my wife to buy. What do you think of that, Miss Pouty Face?" Maura let out a scream and hugged her husband so tightly his back cracked! "Great," he said, "now you've made me a cripple and I'll never be able to work again!" "Can we really afford a big house? How many bedrooms? Wouldn't it be great if it had a big back yard for the boys to play in? Do you think the kitchen will be big? Oh and we'll need a formal dining room". "Maura, you're making me dizzy with all the questions. And I'm deeply hurt that you don't care about my injured back!", Mark joked.

"Well if we have a big kitchen, I can make something more exciting to add to the New Years Dinner than baked French Fries.", Maura retorted. "I like French Fries. Why baked? Sounds boring!" Mark was already contemplating a big plate of fries with tons of ketchup if Maura would let him. "It's not very sophisticated, and I really want to show off some of my Julia Child expertise. Incidentally, they are called Pommes Frites in French and I'm too tired and too busy to really do anything from her book this year.", Maura said after reconsidering all the work that would be involved with doing a Julia Child dish. And as if she had read Mark's mind: "No ketchup at the table on New Years Day! I've invited our neighbors across the street to come. They have a little boy and girl that are around Michael's age and they are so cute playing together." "Fine!", Mark said grudgingly and walked out of the room like a little boy who was just told he couldn't go to Disneyland.

CRUDITES AND SKUNK CAKE

Maura and Mark were now moved into their new home in Lakewood, and Maura loved all of the space they now had. She could even hang her laundry outside to dry and the smell of the clothes blowing dry in the fresh air was intoxicating to her. One day as she was coming in with a bag of freshly dried towels, she was greeted by an excited Michael:

"Mommy, Mommy, look at the new pet I got? Can we keep her?" Maura stopped dead in her tracks, horrified at the sight before her. "Michael, don't move, okay. Mommy is going to find a nice box for…"

It was too late—Michael's new "pet" had become frightened and sprayed that horrendous skunk odor in her beautiful new kitchen. She had to throw all of the laundry out, Michael and her clothes, and pretty much buy all new everything for the kitchen.

Mark had a great laugh at this that evening, but Maura did not find it amusing at all since she was the one who had to throw everything out and attempt to clean all signs of the skunk's presence in their home. Incidentally, the skunk scurried out of the sliding door to the kitchen and was never seen nor heard from again.

"Honey," Mark yelled as he entered their home one Saturday afternoon, "I have the perfect new dish for New Years—Skunk A La King! What do you think?" "You're hysterical, Mark," she replied sarcastically. "Unfortunately, it will have to wait until next year because I've come up with an easy appetizer—Crudites." "What's that? Sounds exotic, and you know I don't like them there foreign foods." Mark was doing his best redneck impression for Maura. "It's just different types of vegetables cut up and served raw.", Maura informed him. "Why don't they just call it raw vegetables—oh mon dieu, crudités sounds more sophisticated." (he this time used a French accent.) "Mark," she said jokingly, "Keep your day job. The accents aren't so great!" "Oh, my Bella Maura, you no likea my accents? Come here! Let me pincha you tush!" Mark was on a roll now.

Actually Maura had already changed her mind about the crudités and decided to bake a chocolate cake with crème Anglais in the filling and a fondant frosting. She really was learning so much from her cookbooks and enjoying experimenting a bit also. Mark had unknowingly given her a great idea. She would make the cake in the shape of a skunk and frost it with black frosting and put white melted marshmallows down its back. It took her awhile to cut out the shape of the cake since no store obviously carried cake pans shaped like a skunk. For almost three hours she perfected her cake and on New Years day she put the finishing touches on it before the company arrived for the big feast. Maura was quite pleased with how it turned out—only problem was no one wanted to eat it because the thought of eating a skunk cake grossed everyone out. Finally one brave soul (Mark) cut a piece and when everyone saw how beautiful it looked inside, they all had some and raved about it.

KINGS CAKE

The years went by and now the boys were both in school and Maura seemed to have a bit more time for herself. She loved driving by the lake and looking at the beautiful mansions that overlooked the water. Someday maybe they would live here, she thought. The eighties had arrived and the unprecedented wealth that many were experiencing (it was the age of the yuppie) had begun to filter down to Mark's air conditioning business.

He had already almost outgrown his plant and had to turn away new business because he was so backlogged. Maura was helping out a couple of days a week and loved interacting with his ever expanding office help. One day one of the bookkeepers told Maura they heard about a great buy in Rocky River. This was so close to the area Maura loved driving by, that she made an appointment to view the house later that day. As soon as she stepped in to the marble foyer with the beautiful spiral staircase, she knew this was her dream house. There had been a death in the family and the owners needed to sell fast, so the price was quite low. Maura had seen enough of what went on at her husband's work to know that the price might not be out of range. She rushed home and made what had become her husband's favorite sweet—the traditional Kings Cake that is served at Mardi Gras in New Orleans. No smell in the world could compare to yeast bread baking in the oven, and Maura timed it so the bread would just be coming out when Mark arrived home. The boys were already in bed (or secretly on the phone with their friends) when Mark walked in the door.

"Uh oh. I smell a major favor to be asked of me!" Mark knew his wife pretty well. "Is that what I think it is?" "Yes, and just because I made Kings Cake doesn't mean I want something in return. I did it because I love you so much, honey." Maura said all of this very facetiously, of course. As Mark cut every piece hoping to get the prize hidden inside the bread with Maura scolding him for doing this, she told him about the dream house she had viewed today. Mark half listened as he devoured three pieces of the pastry ignoring the chicken and broccoli on his plate.

"Babe, this isn't a good time. Mortgage rates are through the ceiling right now, and we just can't afford it. Be patient, someday we'll get there. But on the bright side, I think we have our New Years recipe for next year! I love this stuff.", he said as he forced one more piece down his already bulging belly. Maura didn't argue because she knew he was under a lot of pressure right now with the business expanding faster than they were prepared for. "Seems like a lot of work to do for New Years when we—correction I am already making so many dishes on New Years. But if that's what my man wants, then By God I'll do it!" She loved mocking him sometimes for his total lack of appreciation for the time she put into these New Years meals. But humor always seemed the proper way to go with him.

A few weeks later Mark came home early enough to have dinner with her and the boys (a rare occasion in the

Michaelsons anymore). Mark was very excited and announced that he had found a commercial building that would be more than large enough to accommodate the growing business. "How much is the rent?", Maura asked.

"Oh that's the great part of this, the building is for sale and I already figured out I could rent some of the space that I wouldn't need out to a friend of mine that would help with the mortgage. No more landlords to contend with. No more triple net this and triple net that. I'd be the landlord tacking on all these extra fees." Mark had it all figured out. He had just once again forgot to consult Maura about his plans.

She was beyond furious. Her napkin was thrown on her plate and she ran to the bedroom and slammed the door as hard as she could and locked the door. Ignoring Mark's pleas to open the door, she ranted and cried into her pillow. They couldn't buy the home of her dreams because mortgage rates were too high, but apparently they weren't too high to buy an office building for his business! She began thinking of his selfishness over the years and just kept calling him a pig and punching her pillow. When he wanted to quit his job and start up a business, bingo he did it! When he didn't want to have anymore children and wanted a vasectomy, bingo he did it! When he wanted to buy a bigger office building, bingo he did it! There was no, what do you think, Maura? "No!!!" It was always "him,him,him". She hated him so much right now that she never wanted to look at his ugly, pig face again. "Ever"! At some point that evening she fell asleep exhausted from her anger and frustration. The next morning she woke up and was happy to see he had already left for work (presumably in the same clothes he wore the day before since he was denied access to his bedroom). The anger had subsided somewhat, but the hurt at him once again excluding her from decisions and denying her the one thing she had asked him for had not left her. She did not drive by the lake that day and she ignored the messages from him on the answering machine when she returned from her chores. There was no dinner that evening—she got fast food for the boys and "he" could fend for himself.

As his car pulled into their garage, Maura hurried off to bed once again locking the door behind her. She wasn't as angry as the day before, but still not ready to look at his face (although she no longer referred to it as ugly nor piggish). Surprisingly, Mark made no effort to talk to her and she did not hear any sounds outside the door that would indicate he was looking for something to eat. The television was turned on very softly for awhile and then the lights were out and she heard nothing. It was driving her crazy to know what was going on, but she was far too proud to open the door and be the first one to "give in". When she woke up the next morning, he was already gone and the kids had apparently left without breakfast also. She was starting to feel a little guilty, but definitely not ready to forgive him. As she walked into the kitchen she noticed her real estate agent's card on the table and next to the card a form called a Buyer's Closing Costs sheet. At the top of the form was written the address of her dream home.

Kings Cake was on the New Years table that year—the last year spent in their Lakewood home. Maura felt like the luckiest woman on earth as she prepared for life in their new home.

CRÈME BRULEE

Maura had already met some of her new neighbors in Rocky River even though they had only moved in a month ago. She decided that this New Year's should be shared with old and new friends. Certainly their new formal dining room could accommodate a horde of people. She spent almost as much time shopping for pretty accessories for the table as she did coming up with the new addition to their ever expanding feast. Mark was always working so hard, he rarely contributed much to the dinner and this year told Maura to make whatever she wanted because he was out of inspiration.

"Mark," she called out to him as he sat on the patio reading the Sunday paper. "I was thinking of Crème Brulee." "I was thinking of Schwa dubay", was his reply. "What the hell are you talking about?" "For our New Years addition. Crème Brulee is so popular right now—it's perfect for our new lifestyle." Maura realized it was the middle of summer and she probably should have been a bit more specific with her husband.

"Keeping up with the Joneses, are we? Sounds fine to me even though I still don't know what you're talking about." Mark was pretty engrossed in his newspaper. "It's a custard dessert that you torch to get a beautiful burnt crust on top," she explained. "Oh, I can't wait!" was his sarcastic reply. That year was a momentous one not just because of the new neighbors who joined the celebratory feast, but because Mark nearly burnt the house down trying to torch the dessert!

EMPANADAS

Mark's Aunt Anais paid an unexpected visit to them the following year for Christmas, and was naturally invited to stay for the New Years Dinner. Her actual name was Ann, but she was something of a bon vivant and changed her name legally many years ago. Maura felt very plain standing next to this very glamorous woman, who still dressed for dinner every evening and insisted on a martini with two olives before she could even think of eating. Aunt Anais had lived in pretty much every corner of the world, and was headed for South America to live with a gaucho she met while skiing in Italy earlier in the year. In honor of her upcoming move, Maura and Mark felt it fitting to add a South American treat to the New Years dinner.

"Darling you must let me help with the empanadas. Carlos would be thrilled if I learned how to make at least one dish for him." Aunt Anais wasn't accustomed to being told no, so Maura broke her long tradition of being the only one besides Mark who could make a contribution to the big day.

Michael and Mathew refused to even try the empanadas, which was a little embarrassing for Maura, but everyone else found them extraordinarily yummy! Every year after that, Aunt Anais always sent them a Happy New Years card from whatever section of the globe she happened to be in at the time. (her affair with Carlos lasted a little longer than the time it took she and Maura to make the empanadas that New Years). Maura started a scrapbook of the cards because they were all so unique and interesting.

BLACKENED SNAPPER

This New Years was going to be especially nerve racking for Maura. The Plain Dealer was going to do a little piece on the Michaelsons' New Years Dinner tradition, and everyone who even remotely knew them wanted to come to dinner to hopefully be in the paper. She chose a simple dish, blackened snapper, since it was so popular. Many of the dishes were prepared ahead and frozen so she could be focused on the journalist who would be covering the story that day. When Mark told his employees about the newspaper, they all wanted to come also.

"Mark, we already have almost fifty people for dinner!" Maura protested. "How can we possibly add another ten?" "Can't we just set up another table in the living room?" Poor Mark! He just didn't realize that when the Plain Dealer comes to your home, everything has to be perfect and you cannot have people eating in the living room.

"I'll deal with it, babe." Mark assured her. "I'll just give them a later time to come and hopefully most of the guests will be gone by then."

Maura reluctantly agreed. When the big day arrived, she had everything in the house arranged perfectly, right down to pretty gold ribbons tied around the towels in the guest bathroom. Everything went fairly well and the newspaper people left about an hour after taking pictures. Just as Mark promised, the employees and their families came after most of the guests had already left and Maura made sure there was plenty of food for the new arrivals.

The following day when the story was printed, Maura was horrified to see that the only picture to make the paper was Mark's employees sitting outside in their car with the caption that read "Left out in the cold". Apparently the employees found out what time the dinner really was and cornered the journalist and photographer as they were leaving and told them they had been told not to come to dinner because the Michaelsons' only wanted their well to do friends joining them.

MELON AND PROSCIUTTO

It was now the late eighties, and Maura took gourmet cooking classes at the Rocky River Country Club. Her instructor had just returned from a one month sojourn in Italy and taught them an easy appetizer that was so marvelous! Maura told Mark it would make a great addition to their New Year's feast. She bought a melon baller and scooped out the pretty red balls from the watermelon. An Italian market was not too far away, and they furnished her with the prosciutto so she could practice making it perfect. There was only one tiny problem— where would one purchase watermelon in winter in Cleveland?! Maura's cooking instructor didn't feel the watermelon balls would freeze very well, so Maura gave up on the idea. It was now two weeks before Christmas and she didn't know what to make for this year's New Year. Mark called her from work to tell her the Christmas angel would be paying them a visit this year. Seems one of Mark's clients was going to Brazil and would be returning the day before New Year's. He thought he could pull some strings and bring back a watermelon with him in return for being invited to their home on New Year's day. Who could turn down that offer?! The watermelon wasn't as sweet as what Maura was accustomed to, but all the guests enjoyed the sweet/salty hors'doeuvre.

COSMOPOLITANS

Michael and Mathew were both now in college and Maura was noticing more and more grey hairs on her head. Mark's beer belly was increasing proportionately to his hairs falling out. Ah the joys of middle age! Now that the eighties had come to an end, the great food revolution that swept through that decade also seemed to die down. Maura was watching one of the dopey Hollywood news shows one evening when the Barbie Doll entertainmentcaster mentioned that Cosmopolitans were the new fave rave drink of the stars. Ever since the early years of drinking "fuzzy pussy", Maura had never thought of serving a signature cocktail on New Years Day. A bar was just set up and people helped themselves to what they wanted. This year she decided to limit the drinks to just one, the Cosmopolitan. What could be simpler than cranberry juice and vodka, and she was really running out of room on her table for all the various New Year's dishes that had been multiplying over the years. Mark gave the okay, and Michael and Mathew were thrilled to be included in the adult imbibing part of the day for the first time ever.

ITALIAN DISH THAT CAN'T BE PRONOUNCED

Maura still made frequent visits to the little Italian grocery store where she first purchased prosciutto several years before. It was a family owned business and Mrs. Fabiano, the owner, invited her to have lunch at their home one day. Lunch was a seven course feast that included a heavenly sweet bread stuffed with ham and ricotta cheese and herbs. Maura begged for the recipe, which Mrs. Fabiano obliged her with. It had an unusual Italian name that Maura couldn't even begin to pronounce. After a few attempts at making it, Maura felt it was good enough to add to the following year's New Year's feast. She especially wanted to make a good impression because Michael's fiancée (who was Italian) was coming to meet the family for the first time. Since she wanted to have plenty of time to visit with her prospective daughter-in-law, she made the Italian bread early and froze it. Four days after Christmas, there was a power failure and Maura decided to put the breads out in the snow to keep them frozen. Mathew was instructed to put the breads back in the freezer once the power came on while Maura went shopping to return most of her Christmas presents. Unfortunately, Mathew got a call from his girlfriend and forgot about the breads. When Maura returned from shopping, the breads were totally soggy and not edible. Undaunted, she made a fresh batch the following day and Chiara, Michael's fiancée, loved them.

SUSHI

1995 was a very hectic year with Michael and Chiara's pending wedding and Mathew getting his master's degree. Maura had become quite expert at throwing parties and both Mathew's graduation party and Michael and Chiara's rehearsal dinner came off without a hitch. One of her neighbors made sushi for the graduation party, and of course, Maura had to learn how to make it. She spent two weeks practically camped out at her neighbor's learning the complex and time consuming art of making sushi. She wasn't sure if she could find the time to add it to this year's New Year's table, but decided to give it a try. After 28 years of cooking new items, Maura had to make many of the dishes ahead and freeze them. The sushi had to be made fresh that day (including a dipping sauce which she ended up purchasing). Mark and the boys were in charge of getting the table and bar set up and assembling the various dishes out. Watching bowl games on television was supposed to take a back seat this year, but boys will be boys and Maura ended up doing most of the set up work herself. She had been up since 5 a.m. making sushi and was totally exhausted by noon. Power naps were big these days, so Maura decided to try a quickie nap to refresh herself. After only a few seconds of sleeping Mark was gently shaking her to wake up. All the company was here and the hostess was sound asleep.

"I just fell asleep, can't you let me be for two seconds?", a drowsy Maura asked her husband. "Babe, you've been sleeping for almost two hours and everyone is pretty well plastered by now waiting for you to start eating." Mark replied. Now there was no time to fix herself up properly and when she walked in to the room full of people looking like something the cat had dragged in, Michael took a picture of her and everyone broke out into hysterics.

ROSEMARY PORK LOIN

That year Maura received the best birthday present ever from her three "boys". She was going to Italy for two weeks to take cooking classes from one of the members of the prominent DiMedici family. Mark and the boys would join her for a week after the classes were over. Maura was beside herself with joy! She had never been more than fifty miles outside Cleveland so this was certainly going to be the trip of a lifetime! Italy was more than she could have dreamed it to be, and the classes were great fun and she met people from all over the world (yes, men took the classes also). It was amazing to Maura how simplistic Italian food was, yet so unbelievably wonderful. The kids had joked with her that she would have enough new dishes for New Years that she would never have to wonder what to make for the rest of her life. On the last day of class, they made a roasted pork loin with a little olive oil and fresh rosemary that was the best pork Maura had ever tasted. Of course, this would be on the New Years' menu next year. Once the rest of the family joined her, the real touring began and Maura could not decide which city was the most incredible. She almost cried when it was time to return home, but had memories (and recipes) that she would always treasure. Some good news and bad news came from her memorable trip. The good news was she was going to be a grandmother and finally have the little girl she always so wanted. The bad news? Michael and Chiarra were naming the baby girl Venezia (in honor of where she was conceived). Always trying to look on the bright side, Mark told Maura they should be grateful she wasn't conceived in Stuttgart!

CHOCOLATE VESUVIUS CAKE

Little Venezia came into the world on a bitter cold wintry day in February. Mark and Maura couldn't even make it to the hospital because there was a blizzard and the roads were far too dangerous. Once the blizzard cleared a bit they finally got to see their beautiful little granddaughter with the horrible first name. Maura had bought her several frilly little dresses that she would eventually grow into and had bought a years' supply of diapers and baby bottles. Venezia was allergic to her mother's milk and most formulas and had to drink goat's milk for the first three months of her life. The poor little thing was constantly having diarrhea and Maura worried that she wasn't getting enough nutrition. She suggested that Michael and Chiarra have a day off from the baby and she would watch her. Spring had finally arrived and she thought it might be fun to take Venezia for a little walk in her stroller. Mark came home early from work that day and offered to take care of their little princess while Maura ran to the store to pick up a few things she forgot the day before. She rushed through her shopping so Mark wouldn't have to be alone with the baby for too long. When she came home, Mark had an exasperated look on his face and excrement on his arms and hands. Despite her best efforts, Maura burst out laughing.

"They should have named her Vesuvius instead of Venezia, because the poop just keeps erupting from her every two seconds!", Mark was obviously not enjoying his babysitting experience much. "But isn't she beautiful, Mark?" Maura was trying to change his focus a bit. Mark just scowled and handed Venezia over to Maura while he cleaned himself up.

"Mark, you just gave me the inspiration for next year's dish. I'm going to make a chocolate Vesuvius cake in honor of our little doll!" Maura was already planning how to have chocolate erupt from the fudge cake she would make. Everyone marveled at the cake that year, until Mark told them how it came about. There were lots of groans after his story, but no one stopped eating!

BELLINIS

The final year of the century was so hectic for Maura. Chiarra went back to work so Maura watched little Venezia three times a week. In addition to helping out at Mark's office twice a week, Maura had recently taken up golf so spent as much time as possible on perfecting her golf swing. The year raced by and neither Mark nor Maura had given any thought to what would be added to this year's New Years' table. Maura decided to recreate the wonderful peach bellini she had at Harry's Bar in Venice during her marvelous trip to Italy. She made a huge pitcher of them and even poured some of the peach nectar into her ice cube trays so the ice didn't dilute the drinks. Naturally they were a big hit with the ever-expanding crowd of guests.

COCONUT AMARETTO CAKE

Michael and Chiarra had invited everyone to dinner for a big announcement in February. They would also be celebrating Venezia's birthday and this would actually be the first birthday that Venezia would have some cognizance of what was going on. Wagers were started on what the big announcement would be—Mark thought Michael was making a career change (something he had been considering for quite some time). Maura was certain they were going to provide Venezia with a little sister or brother (hopefully with a normal name). Mathew and his girlfriend both thought either Michael or Chiarra had a job transfer out of the area (not very appealing so that idea was quickly vetoed by Mark and Maura). When the evening arrived, everyone was full of anticipation and could hardly wait for Venezia to open her presents after dinner and birthday cake to hear the big news. As it turned out, they only wanted to tell everyone that Venezia was going to be baptized. Mark and Maura tried to pretend they were excited, but secretly were disappointed that the big news wasn't more momentous. Since all four of the gamblers lost the bet, no one had to pay up so at least the announcement wasn't a total disappointment. The baptism occurred in early April and the whole family went to brunch afterwards on Chiarra's uncle's beautiful yacht. It was quite a spread, and a beautiful cake was brought out to honor the newly baptized little girl. It had coconut and amaretto in it, but Maura was unsuccessful in getting the recipe from the caterer. She decided to try to recreate it for the following New Years. After a couple of failed attempts, she came up with a most delicious cake (even better than what they had on the yacht that day) and she formed the cake in the shape of a cross to honor Venezia's baptism. What a comedic sight seeing the skunk and cross cake side by side on the dessert table on New Year's Day.

STUFFED ARTICHOKES

2001 hadn't progressed very far when Maura got some unbelievably exciting news—a publisher had contacted her about possibly writing a cookbook based on her New Year's day recipes. There were so many details to be worked out, but Maura was thrilled beyond belief at her good fortune. So many really talented writers spend years honing their craft and attempting to get published, and she had someone seeking out her write a book! Borrowing on Michael and Chiarra's idea, Maura asked both boys to come over that Sunday afternoon for lunch. She told no one (not even Mark) about her big news. After lunch was over and dessert was being brought out, Maura decided to make her big announcement. Before she had a chance to say anything, Mathew stood up and clinked his glass to announce he wanted to propose a toast.

"I'd like everyone to raise their glasses." Mathew said nothing else, so everyone raised their glasses and started giggling waiting for the rest of the toast. Finally after a few seconds, Mathew continued: "Now I'd like everyone to pass their glass to the person on their left."

This was greeted with more laughter and questions about what was going on and why didn't he just pour the champagne and stop all the games. However, everybody eventually dutifully obeyed the toastmaster and passed their empty glass to the left. Suddenly Mathew's girlfriend, Noreen, let out a shriek. She jumped up and hugged Mathew, as she clutched the 3 carat diamond ring that he had secretly placed inside the glass she now was holding. After several minutes of hugging, kissing and congratulating things calmed down and the champagne was finally poured. Maura didn't want to steal her son and his new bride-to-be's thunder so she decided to say nothing about her book. After several glasses of champagne and some unsurpassed giddiness on everyone's part, Maura changed her mind and sheepishly announced (in somewhat slurred words) that she was going to be a published author. More rounds of hugging, kissing and congratulating ensued (not to mention more glasses of champagne to be consumed). It was probably one of the most special days of their lives, and unfortunately they all were too intoxicated to remember much of it the next day! 2001 was definitely going to be a very good year (as Frank Sinatra liked to say). Once the excitement of the book and upcoming wedding wore off, Maura found that she was totally drained preparing her recipes, babysitting Venezia and working for Mark. Golf was sadly neglected so she could focus on other matters. Thankfully, Mathew and Noreen decided to have a small wedding and Maura didn't need to be too involved in the planning. Once Maura set up a regular routine on working on her book, she found it enjoyable and felt she was the luckiest person in the world. How many other women were going to have a published book in addition to having a wonderful, loving husband and two sons who were happy and in love? Then September 11th came, and no one's life was ever quite the same. Noreen's cousin was in the twin towers that horrible morning, but managed to get out of the building unharmed. Mark's former customer who had just recently relocated to New York wasn't as fortunate. One day when Maura was watching Venezia, she prepared artichokes and Venezia was able to pronounce the name of the vegetable almost perfectly which astounded Maura. Maura decided to stuff the artichokes with some cheese and mushrooms and anchovies and that would be the new addition to the New Year's table for the following year.

STUFFED AVOCADO

Everyone in the ever-expanding Michaelson family looked forward to the new year and putting the great tragedy of 9/11 behind them. Mathew stopped by unexpectedly in the middle of the day and told his mother that he wasn't sure the marriage to Noreen would come about. Because she was Catholic, they were required to go to pre-nuptial classes before they could be married in the church. Noreen had never mentioned that any children they might have would need to be raised Catholic until the subject came up at their pre-nuptial classes. Perhaps if she had told him from the beginning, Mathew would not have objected, or at least he could have made a logical decision about continuing the relationship. But now he felt betrayed and was very angry that she never mentioned what she had to have known all along. Maura knew it was best to not say anything against Noreen in case the storm blew over and the wedding went on as scheduled. After venting for what seemed like an eternity to Maura, Mathew finally calmed down and agreed to stay for dinner. Since Mark was working late, Maura hadn't even thought about what to have, so she decided to make a crab salad and stuff it in an avocado.

"I sure miss your cooking, Mom." Mathew said sadly. "You should give Noreen some of your recipes, or better yet, have her come over and give her a cooking lesson or two.", he continued.

Maura smiled at her son as they both realized that the love he felt for his beautiful fiancée could overcome any anger he felt toward her. Someone had told Maura once that crab is an aphrodisiac, so she always wondered if that was the turning point for Mathew. Of course, she knew it wasn't but she decided right then and there to make this same dish next New Year's Day to hopefully spark some renewed interest from her husband. Again she smiled at this thought.

Noreen and Mathew's wedding was so lovely and Maura felt that she was sitting on top of the world. Her cookbook was almost finished, both of her sons were now happily married, and her husband was hopefully going to get a little jolt to his libido this New Year's from a crab salad!

2003

A premonition of the horrible year ahead hit Maura when her apron caught on fire right before the guests arrived for the big feast. Fortunately Mark was there and put it out immediately. A few months later, Maura received a call from her book agent that the publishing company had filed Chapter 11 and part of the reorganization was to put on hold any future books not written by known artists. Maura was crushed, and talked to Mark about finding another publisher. Michael suggested that she self-publish the book.

Noreen suffered a miscarriage shortly after getting pregnant, and Mathew blamed himself for some strange reason. And then on June 11th, her husband came home early from work and delivered the ultimate blow. To say that Maura was shocked that her husband had been diagnosed with cancer would be a huge understatement. His surgery was scheduled for the very next day and all the family sat vigil for the one and one half hour procedure. The doctors were very encouraging and felt the chemo would knock out any remaining bad cells that could still be there. Mark never lost his sense of humor nor his optimism. Perhaps that is more important than the poisonous drugs the doctors wanted to inject him with. After three weeks he was back at work, refusing to follow the doctor's program and doing his own thing instead. And now fast forward five months and Maura was nervously waiting for Mark to return home from his follow up MRI. She tried desperately to keep busy that morning with grocery shopping and cleaning and calling a few of her golf buddies. She vainly tried not looking at the clock, but every time she did she felt more butterflies in her stomach. Why hadn't he called from his cell as she asked him to do? He didn't want her to go to the appointment with him, and now she was kicking herself for abiding by his wishes. Finally she couldn't stand it anymore and dialed his cell. When the phone began to ring, she was startled until she realized it was Mark's cell that was ringing. In his haste to leave that morning, he forgot to bring his cell. All she could do was hope he'd call from a pay phone. Now every two minutes she would look at the clock. She called her two sons but neither had heard from their father. Perhaps she could do some gardening to calm herself down? As she went to grab her big gardening hat, she heard the garage door open. Her heart felt as though it would jump out of her body at any minute it was pounding so hard. She heard the car door shut and she was waiting in the kitchen for him to walk in. After what seemed like ten hours he opened the door from the garage. Eagerly she searched his face for some indication of how his MRI went, but saw nothing.

"Babe, I'm sorry to tell you this," he began. Maura felt as if her life had just been drained from her. "But you're not going to be able to spend that life insurance money for probably a long time." And a sheepish grin crossed his face. "You asshole" Maura screeched as she jumped into his arms. All the pent up emotion she had felt for the last six months exploded as she cried and laughed and hugged her husband as tight as she possibly could. "Uh, babe", her most wonderful husband said, "I think you just crushed my ribs and now I won't be able to work for a month!"

"Always with the jokes, this guy!" Maura was so happy and thankful and relieved and hungry! She realized she hadn't eaten all morning because she was so nervous so she made both of them a peanut butter and jelly sandwich and they both had a good laugh at her "gourmet" luncheon.

A couple of days later over dinner, Maura told Mark that she had an idea for this New Year's Day. Noreen had told her that her church had an office set up to distribute food to the disadvantaged.

"What if we skip doing the New Year's thing this year and instead take food to the needy in the area. We have so much to be thankful for and I think we need to give back to the community. Would you be terribly disappointed if we didn't have our New Year's feast just this once?", she timidly asked her husband. Mark thought it was a splendid idea. It was very difficult calling all their guests to tell them they would not be having New Years this year, but everyone was very understanding if not a little disappointed.

So on January 1, 2004, for the first time in thirty-five years, Mark and Maura Michaelson spent all morning driving to the homes that weren't as fortunate as theirs, and providing bags full of groceries to these people instead of having a lavish feast in their own beautiful house. Mark and Maura had never been happier and decided to make this a Thanksgiving (they couldn't give up their famed New Years every year) tradition from now on. On the way home, Michael called to invite them over for a bite to eat. Maura hated to put Noreen out since she was now six months pregnant, but reluctantly agreed. When

Mathew and Noreen opened the front door for their parents, there was a whole houseful of people yelling "Happy New Year" at the Michaelsons as they entered the living room. It was all the friends and family who had enjoyed New Years Day over the years with the Michaelsons. And on a very long table in the living room was every dish and drink that Mark and Maura had ever served for New Years Day!

UNCLE NATHAN'S WEDDING

Maura stared at the invitation for a few seconds trying to comprehend the letters on the pretty lavender paper. "Mark, does your Aunt Anais have a daughter named Anais?", she yelled this to Mark who was watching a tennis match in the other room. "Not that I know of, babe.", he replied hoping that would be the end of the discussion so he could go back to match point. "She must, are you sure? Maybe you just never heard of her. Aunt Anais did have quite a few husbands, right?", Maura was determined to engage her husband in conversation. "I don't know of any kids. As I recall there were some stepchildren in a couple of her unions." Mark was hoping that was the end of the discussion, but he knew it was like hoping for money from the tooth fairy after you're grown up. "Well would she have named any of the stepchildren after herself?" Maura was getting more and more curious about this most unusual woman. "Honey, it's match point, can we discuss this later?" Mark was trying not to sound annoyed. "How many more innings before it's over?" Maura had difficulty keeping Mark's sports straight. "It's tennis!" After thirty some years of marriage she still didn't know anything about his sports which occasionally irritated the beejesus out of him.

"We were invited to the wedding of Anais Doverly. That

wasn't your Aunt Anais's last name so it must be her daughter.",
Maura persisted. Now Mark was a little curious also and
decided to join his wife to take a peek at the invite. Mark
opined that she probably had divorced Andrew McCarthy, (the
last husband they were aware of) and remarried this Doverly
fellow and forgot to sign her new name on her most recent
Christmas card. Maura said that no woman is that absent
minded to forget her new husband—although many would
like to.

"The Honour of your presence is requested at the marriage
of Anais Doverly to Nathan Michael Mathers," Mark read
aloud. Mark decided to make some phone calls and soon found
out that it was, in fact, his octogenarian aunt who was walking
down the aisle once again. Well as Mathew would say, Aunt
Anais has it going on!

Cynthia wasn't terribly surprised when the invitation
arrived in the mail. Between her mother and her sister, she
was well aware that love was in the air back in Connecticut.
She wondered what sort of woman would even consider being
in the same room with that old goat, much less want to marry
him. What did surprise her was they were getting married at
the Samuel Duvalier estate. Sarah had always raved about the
place and it cost beaucoup bucks to have any function there.
Not only had Uncle Nathan found an insane woman to marry
him, he found a rich, insane woman!

Lenny was going over some last minute instructions with
his head chef when he got the call from Anais. She had been
a regular customer at his restaurant in the early days and had
persuaded all of her influential friends into being regulars there
also. Lenny was truly sad when she told him she was divorcing
her husband and moving to Thailand. Over the years after
she left, she would always send him Christmas cards from
wherever she happened to be living at the time (which usually
depended on whom she happened to be bedding at the time).
Of course, Lenny told her he'd be honored to cater her wedding,

even if it meant taking most of his crew to Connecticut. She assured him money was no object, and Lenny had no difficulty believing that, based on the lifestyle and acquaintances she had in Savannah during her stay. Holly, who had settled into Savannah life quite well by now, was thrilled at the prospect of returning to the area she had frequented during her marriage with many of her friends and happily agreed to accompany Lenny to the wedding.

So on a beautiful June day, two hundred guests assembled at the Samuel Duvalier Estate to witness the union of Aunt Anais and Uncle Nathan. Cynthia had brought along her old pal, Nikki, (now once again married to an Austrian diplomat at the United Nations) to ensure the wedding came off perfectly Scott had a gig that weekend and couldn't come so Cynthia was hoping Nikki would be her date. Unfortunately once the ceremony was over and the reception was just beginning, Nikki took off to catch a plane to New York to be with her new husband. Since there wasn't enough room at the bridal table, Cynthia agreed to sit at the "odd man out" table. Just as she was taking her seat, a pretty woman whom Cynthia thought was probably in her mid-thirties sat down next to her and introduced herself as Holly. Her boyfriend was catering the dinner so Holly would be alone most of the afternoon and evening also. An annoying divorcee in his 50's, a widower in his 80's and a couple most likely in their early 60's completed the "odd man out" table. Since the widower's hearing aid wasn't working well, and the divorcee spent more time at the bar than at their table, Cynthia, Holly and the other couple, the Michaelsons, got acquainted and began really enjoying each other's company immensely. At one point while Maura and Mark were dancing, Cynthia noticed Holly fidgeting with her fingers. Apparently she was trying to remove a ring from her finger and having some difficulty doing so.

Cynthia: "That's some rock you've got there. Rubies were always my favorite!"

Holly smiled shyly and her face turned about the same color as the huge jewel she was sporting. "I meant to put the ring on my other finger this morning and forgot and now I can't get it off. The heat must have made my fingers swell." Cynthia was curious why she wanted to switch the ring to her right hand. Holly pleaded with her not to tell anyone but whispered in her ear that it was an engagement ring. "That's not anything to keep quiet about. A ring that big and beautiful has to be paraded around." Cynthia exclaimed. "I just don't want to steal any thunder from the bride. It's her day." Holly was the sweetest girl, but enough is enough. "That old bag has been married more times than probably everyone in this room put together." Cynthia joked. "You don't have to hide this from anyone. But I'll respect your privacy and not grab the mike and announce it to everyone if you promise to tell me every teeny detail."

Even though the two women had just met, a real bond had formed and Cynthia was truly happy and excited for her new friend. They were so deep in conversation that they hadn't noticed that the Michaelsons had returned from the dance floor. "Ohhh, it's gorgeous" Maura exclaimed as she noticed the ring for the first time. Mark, feeling obviously out of place, excused himself from the table so the three women could talk their boring girl talk. Cynthia and Maura had tears in their eyes as they heard the story of the young lovers reunited after so many years and now ready to form their family again. The conversation eventually turned to Maura and how she was proposed to which eventually turned to their New Years feasts. Both of the other women were immediately invited to fly to Ohio for the following New Year and both readily accepted.

Their conversation had a brief interruption when the newlyweds came to their table to exchange pleasantries. Cynthia chuckled silently at the thought of poor old Uncle Nathan having to be polite to people all day, but she did see a side of him she had never noticed before—he was actually semi-human!

Holly and the Michaelsons went over to the cake table to watch the bride and groom cut the cake. Cynthia decided to sit it out and maybe make a quick call to Scott while everyone else was distracted. Unfortunately it went in to his voicemail so she decided not to leave a message. As she hung up the phone she caught the tail end of Aunt Anais toasting her husband (thankfully she didn't mention that she hoped they would live a long and happy life together because really, who's kidding who here?)

Aunt Anais: "So thank all of you adorable dears for traveling so far to see my Nate Nate and I declare our undying love for each other forever and ever." Cynthia was just getting ready to toss her cookies when Aunt Anais said something that quickly made her sit up very straight in her chair. "And leave some room for the wonderful cookies that my most famous stepson baked for our special occasion today. The waiters are wheeling the cookie cart in right now and I can't wait for a taste of these divine morsels!" Aunt Anais announced in her most dramatic, affected tone.

Out of curiosity, Cynthia walked over to the cookie tray. Surely the famous stepson couldn't be the same cookie baker that Cynthia had gone out with so long ago! But as soon as she spotted some of the cookies, she immediately recognized the sugary concoctions that had tasted beyond anything she had ever had before or since. There were many familiar cookies on the table and some new ones that she hadn't tried. As Anais was making her way through the crowd, Cynthia asked if her stepson was here today and was relieved to hear he had prior commitments and had shipped the cookies in that morning.

She decided to try one of the never sampled cookies and as she placed a bite in her mouth, she closed her eyes to savor every second of the ecstasy. As the chocolate goo melted on her tongue, a huge smile erupted from her lips. Then, suddenly it felt like a dark cloud had swept across the sun to block its rays. "Looks like you've got that taste bud disease under control!" And she opened her eyes to see that the "dark cloud" was actually the man who had baked the cookies!